Praise for The Quantum Curators

'A protagonist who complains about British weather is one thing, but one who feels the Thames would be much improved by a few crocodiles is something else!'

'Some genuinely laugh out loud m⁓ of characters, and a meta plot tha⁓ the next one!'

'...a fun take, with engaging chara⁓

'... funny, bloody hilarious in place⁓
I think, if the next one is as good, it will be the start of a bloody good series of books.'

Amazon

'A very entertaining, action-packed read with excellent characters and several good jokes - and no doubt some more I missed :) Reminiscent of *Ash* by Mary Gentle and the *Rivers of London* series.'

'...a delightfully fun read.'

'St. John does a great job of weaving in real history with fiction and an alternative history. So much fun!'

'It started interesting and just got better. The twists were unexpected and added to the story, can't wait for the next instalment.'

'Enjoyable and quirky.'

Good Reads

By Eva St. John

THE
QUANTUM CURATORS
AND THE
FABERGÉ EGG

EVA ST. JOHN

MUDLARK'S PRESS

First published 2020 by Mudlark's Press

First paperback edition 2020
ISBN 9781913628017 (paperback)
ISBN 9781913628024 (large print)

www.thequantumcurators.com

#1 Neith – Beta Earth

'Has she chucked the bloody thing in the lake yet?'

My earpiece hissed. 'No, hang on. Oh, you are *not* going to like this.' Clio started sniggering. 'Some of our intel may be wrong.'

I didn't need to be able to see Clio to know that her eyes were rolling. *Patchy intel* was our stock in trade. Especially the further back in time we had to go. Seventh-century Britain was about as patchy as it got. It was a wonder sometimes how a culture collapsed in on itself. One minute, Roman rules, the next, hello Dark Ages. And not so much dark, as, for fuck's sake, you used to have underfloor heating, how could you let that go?

Still, there were shining pockets of artistic wonder. However, they were then generally burnt, plundered, melted down or, in this case, dumped in a lake. Chucking stuff in water seemed to be a bizarre form of preservation, but then again, nothing about the British ever made sense.

'So, what don't we know?' I whispered. From where I was crouched, behind a large rock dripping in wet moss, I had no clear line of sight, so was relying on Clio who was sitting two miles back with her goggles on zoom.

'Turns out these priestesses can't throw swords worth a damn. She lobbed it a whole foot.'

'Bugger, I'd love to have seen that.'

'Watch it on replay later and be bloody glad you didn't. You'd have laughed out loud.'

Well, that explained the group of birds that had suddenly flown up into the sky over on the far ridge above the lake. I had wondered if a second extraction team had been sent over. God knows it wouldn't be the first time a screw up had occurred.

The great Petersburg debacle of 1894 was still taught to first years as a salutary reminder of how *not* to explore a gunpowder factory. The first lesson was how to establish all friendly personnel in the vicinity. The second lesson, which seemed a surprisingly obvious one, was not to use combustible weapons in a fireworks factory. You'd think the curators of the Library of Alexandria would have been more attuned to fire-provoking situations. But hey, it's not like the library caught fire or anything. Oh, wait...

'What are they doing now?'

'There was a lot of undignified arm waving and shouting, then two of the priestesses went and dragged a boat down to the lakeside. Now they're all getting into the boat, with the sword.'

'Shit. Shit! Don't say it.' Clio was not about to let me forget this. She had specifically mentioned the SCUBA gear, and I had just as specifically pooh-poohed it. Bugger. I looked at my rubber boots. Well, they were a waste of time.

'Did you at least pack the lungs?'

'Yes,' I said. I knew what I had to do. Dammit. I was going to be a laughing stock when I got home.

'Well, go fetch Lot DL278643.'

'Can you not just call it Excalibur?'

'That's sloppy. Now strip.'

I was not in a good mood as I peeled off my layers on the cold and wet hillside with the wind blowing the rain into my face. Everything was making me bad tempered, including the stupid nomenclature of our system. The whole point of our organisation was that we retrieved the one-offs, the last of their kind, the unique pieces. They all had sodding names. If there were more than one of them, we wouldn't bother saving them. But no, for some reason, saving Excalibur, the legendary sword of the totemic warlord Arthur, would be better identified as item DL278643. Whatever.

I bit down on the portable bottled air we nicknamed *lungs* and slunk down to the water's edge. My skin was already covered in gooseflesh and my knickers and bra were hardly going to keep me warm, so I stripped those off as well. Next I emptied my utility belt, then filled it with stones and clipped it around my waist. If the people in the little boat glanced to their right, they might have spotted me, so I lay on my belly and pulled myself into the black water. Rocks and pebbles scratched my torso until the water became deep enough for me to start swimming freely. The rocks held me under the flat, inky surface as I kept my teeth clamped around my small re-breather.

'Head northeast,' sounded Clio's voice in my ear, loud amongst the silence of the dark lake.

I'd have replied, but obviously, my mouth was full. Tapping on my wrist piece, I texted her a quick thumbs up and began to swim at speed to intercept the boat. I had an hour of air, but there was no point in risking it. Besides, I was cold. The quicker we finished this extraction, the better. I checked my little computer again. The light was even worse this far down and I tapped on the torch function.

'Oh, nice effect. You've turned the lake a glowing green. Hang on… yep, they're rowing towards you.'

My buoyancy was a perfect counterbalance, about three feet below the surface. I hung in the water and waited for instructions. It's fair to say that waiting for instructions isn't a particular speciality of mine. In fact, it's one of the reasons I was constantly passed over for promotion. It was felt that I wouldn't bring a positive influence to the key functions of the senior management structure. Which suited me just fine. But sometimes you had to rely on others, and if there was one person into whose hands I would willingly entrust my life, it was Clio. Unlike me, she had regularly been offered promotion. Although obviously not in personnel. That wasn't her skill set, which is why I was team leader. Other than that, the girl was a wunderkind. But she too loved being out in the field, so we'd stuck together. Most retrieval units worked in pairs, though sometimes a couple of pairs would work together if it was a complicated extraction. Occasionally, there'd be a solo worker. One who no one else could work with. They did well enough, but they could be total pains in the arse as well. They were usually long in the tooth and spent all their time telling us that back in their day blah blah blah. I have no time for lone wolf bravado.

'Okay, they're almost with you. Start your ascent now.'

Very carefully, I began kicking upwards. I knew the folklore for this event. It was essential that only my forearm broke the surface. Cold air blew across my fingers and I opened my palm. I was tempted to beckon with my finger, but I thought that might be too silly.

'Oh wow. They are freaking out. Stay still, they're turning towards you. Get ready.'

The next moment I felt a hard pommel in my hand, and I wrapped my fingers around it. The second they released it, both me and the sword plunged to the bottom of the lake.

'That wasn't very graceful. You okay?'

No, I was not okay. My arm had nearly been wrenched from its socket and I had to drag the wretched thing out of the soft mud that lined the bottom of the lake. This was how it was lost, simple silt and evaporation. Within only a few years this land would begin to dry up, old lake pits would be filled in and levelled up, and eventually, Excalibur would sit under many metres of earth and tarmac, never to be seen again. Cue me.

I began walking along the lake bed, dragging the stupid noble sword behind me and swearing at every step. At only five foot, I wasn't much taller than the sword itself. I'd had to switch my torch off and now I was stubbing my bare feet on every branch and rock that littered the floor. At one point an eel slithered past my leg and I almost spat my lungs out. Pausing to regain my wits, I continued to trudge to the water's edge.

'Hold your position. They're tying up the boat and heading towards their cart. I'll let you know when they're over the brow of the hill. I'm heading your way now.'

I stood there, head still beneath the icy surface, shivering and cursing. This was one of my most tedious extractions ever. Where were the ropes, the guns, the fights, the chases? That was the sort of extraction I enjoyed, grabbing the item from the flame, outrunning a volcano, snatching it from gangsters. It was not shivering in a dark bog of a lake, waiting for some wafty priestesses, with a proclivity for dumping precious artefacts into lakes, to slowly trundle away.

'Out you come.'

A few more steps and I emerged from the water, removing the breathers from my mouth. 'Next time let's factor in the weight of the retrieval item, shall we?'

Clio laughed at me. 'Holy cow, Neith. Wait 'til you see yourself on the replay. You look like the creature from the black lagoon.'

She untangled me from the pondweed that I'd

accumulated and took the sword from me. No slacker at the bench press, she also grunted in surprise at the sheer weight of it.

'Crap. Yep, see your point. Get dressed and we'll step back. No point in stepping back naked.' Nudity wasn't an issue in our culture, but I didn't need to give the guys a free laugh.

'Not very showy, is it? I was expecting more bling.'

We both looked at the sword. It was a beast of a weapon. I suppose anything capable of hacking through a body didn't also need to sparkle.

I pulled on my trousers and was grateful for the wicking liner that absorbed the water. Being clammy would have been the final insult. With my jacket zipped up, we prepared to leave.

'Protocols. Wrap the blade in the blanket, keep the tip on the floor and your hand on the pommel. On the count of five, step through after me.'

I agreed and prepared the sword. Step through protocols were essential. The quantum functions of the field were normally the same for both parties, but sometimes things went wrong. People were known to come through hours apart, and sometimes they arrived on top of each other. Early efforts had shown that being attached to another human didn't always work. The first person that stepped back discovered they were holding a hand. The second person stepped back screaming their head off with arterial blood pumping out on the floor. One time, an archivist had to come through at a run with their dagger still pointing forward. They impaled the section chief, who had died instantly. Hence all the protocols. Often the most dangerous parts of the extraction were not the volcanoes, earthquakes, or the gangsters, but the simple laws of quantum mechanics. Anything could happen, and usually did.

'Ready?'

I nodded. We both tapped in the recall code, and then she was gone. Five seconds later, so was I.

#2 Julius – Beta Earth

Julius Strathclyde glanced up from his desk as someone loudly proclaimed their arrival at the far end of the Fitzwilliam Museum's acquisitions department. Julius could only think of one person so lacking in the social conventions of the workplace: Charles Bradshaw. If Julius hadn't gone to school with him they'd probably never have been friends, they were so chalk and cheese. He smiled inwardly, thanking fate. Charlie might be colossally annoying at times, but he was still his best friend. It was just that, as always, his timing was appalling.

He sighed as he checked his watch. There were three more box files to catalogue, and he was looking forward to a particularly knotty issue of provenance in the second box. There was no way Charlie was just going to sit quietly and wait whilst he did that. Hopefully, he was simply popping by to say hello.

'Julie, my boy!' Charlie slapped his hands on the desk, causing other researchers to glare in annoyance. 'Come on, I'm here to spring you from your dungeon.'

Julius rolled his eyes. Charlie was a bright guy, so why couldn't he remember how much he detested that nickname? However, Julius was due to go for drinks with Rebecca later on. If he got stuck into the catalogues now, he might lose track of time, and Rebecca didn't approve of tardiness. Losing track of time showed a lack of foresight. If you knew something was going to be interesting, she believed, then you should allot more time to it. Julius' problem was that he never knew what was going to be interesting until he opened the box. If he went for a drink with Charlie now, he wouldn't get lost in his research and let Rebecca down. After telling Charlie to pipe down, he filled in the chits saying the boxes remained uncatalogued, then sent them back to the stacks.

Julius had come to Cambridge to get his degree, and stayed for his fellowship and doctorate. Primarily, he was a research professor at Emmanuel College; his field of study was theology and philosophy of religions, with a specialism in folklore. It paid well enough for his needs, but he supplemented his wage by working part time in the Fitzwilliam as an archivist in the acquisitions department. The money was okay, but he would have been just as happy to do the work for free. There was no better way to spend his time than sat at a desk tracking down a footnote or establishing a provenance. He secretly thought of himself as an Indiana Jones of the library stacks.

He laughed, thinking about his school friend, who was more an Indiana Jones figure in real life. Charlie was a freelancer working for a variety of prestigious museums. He would go out into the field, purchasing various items or travelling with certain collections. His portfolio was loose enough that he never got bored. There was one principal difference between the two men; Charlie went out and acquired the stuff from the darkest corners of the globe, while Julius waited until someone placed it in front of him.

As the two men stepped out onto the street, they were almost immediately accosted by a pod of cyclists. In the narrow mediaeval streets of Cambridge, a bicycle was easily the quickest way to get around, and indeed most of the buses and lorries had been banned from the centre of town.

Walking along the street, they attracted the usual second glances from giggling students and tourists alike. Normally, Charlie would preen, knowing the world was his oyster. A tall, blond, former rower, he regularly turned heads with his good looks and cheerful smile. Standing next to Julius though, he couldn't guarantee the looks were meant for him. There was no getting away from the fact that Julius was a particularly handsome man.

When he had first started school, his blue eyes had peeked out from below a dark floppy fringe. Yet the soft winsome features of a boy sharpened as he became a teenager, and his bone structure solidified into something you could chisel. In Charlie's eyes, Julius' only redeeming features were that he was rubbish at sport, and had absolutely no comprehension of his good looks.

Julius believed what he looked like was completely irrelevant. If anything, at times it could be a misleading hindrance. He'd noticed early on in his studies that people didn't take him quite as seriously as some of the other scholars. He remembered hearing a female model once complaining that no one listened to her because of her looks. He had promptly bought her a drink, and the two of them had got into a lengthy debate on string theory. His friends had hoped that may have been the start of something beautiful, but there had been no chemistry, just academic attraction. Indeed, they still kept in touch, but only to discuss the latest theories or discoveries.

Julius had begun to walk towards the King's Arms, a rowdy sports pub that Charlie favoured, when Charlie suggested the Old Fox instead. They made their way to a quiet corner of the pub, then Julius ordered two pints of beer and some pork scratchings before the pair of them settled down into the booth.

'So, Julie, how's it hanging? It's been months since I saw you.'

Julius mumbled non-committedly. No matter how interested Charlie was, he had something he wanted to tell Julius about. Julius loved to hear his friend's adventures come to life. As he had chosen the Old Fox, Charlie obviously had a good tale to tell, so Julius settled down to be entertained. Sure enough, once Julius mentioned his plans for the weekend with Rebecca, Charlie nodded, then with great enthusiasm, promptly started to talk about himself.

'The new exhibition? It's fascinating. I helped curate that when it opened in Rome. Well worth a visit. Check out the priest's head-piece. Some idiot had actually labelled it as a sword hilt, if you can believe that? I said to Claude, "Claude, I can't possibly put my name to this exhibition if you're going to let that error be made public." He was incredibly grateful. God, imagine the embarrassment?'

Charlie continued to reveal ways in which he had saved the day, and Julius' mind began to wander. Sipping on his beer, he wondered if he could cross-check the provenance with the auction catalogues held in the Courtauld Institute.

'…but that wasn't the most interesting thing about it!'

Julius quickly replayed the last few minutes: a grateful cardinal, a canoe trip in Borneo, malarial antidote, two sisters and some absinthe, a wooden codex, a child's toy. *A child's toy. That was the last thing he'd mentioned. What had been interesting about that?*

'You don't say?' Julius said, playing for time.

'Inside was a note saying, *The first doll has the egg.*'

Julius was struggling to keep up. He couldn't remember what the toy was. 'No, I'm sorry you've lost me.' He tried to piece together everything that Charlie had been saying in the past few minutes. There was a Russian doll's house, maybe, something about a doll having an egg and a note in Russian. Julius was lost.

Charlie banged his pint on the table. 'What do you think, hey?' Having made the announcement, he headed back to the bar for another round of drinks whilst Julius thought over what he had said.

A note about an egg hidden in a Russian doll might mean anything. But it was impossible not to rush to the obvious conclusion. A Fabergé egg.

'Well, what do you say to that?' Charlie returned to the table and placed a second pint in front of Julius.

'Tell me again about the toy.'

'I was in Poland visiting the new exhibition on Lost Childhoods and I got chatting to this little babushka. She said she'd offered to sell an old matryoshka set to the museum but they weren't interested. Well, you know me. I'm always one to have a look. And I'm a sucker for Russian nesting dolls.'

Julius raised an eyebrow. Charlie was a well-known dealer in museum-quality artefacts, but sometimes he sailed very close to the line regarding stolen antiquities and pillaged sites. Charlie was never one to turn down a back-alley deal or an interesting lead.

He had caused an absolute stink in Iraq the previous year when he was found to have a Mesopotamian vase on him that he was apparently in the process of returning to the Iraqi Embassy. The problem was that he was in the airport at the time, heading home to the UK. The British Museum vouched for him, saying they were preparing to authenticate and preserve it, but there were some very uncomfortable conversations on both sides.

Julius took a swig of beer and motioned for Charlie to continue. The pub was beginning to fill as the office workers arrived for a quick drink before heading home.

'Well, we went back to her flat, where she pulled out as fine a samovar as you'd be likely to see outside of a museum, and started to make tea. Her flat was a little cavern of treasures. Every sideboard was full of trinkets, every wall covered in paintings and mirrors and hangings. It was really quite marvellous. Anyway, she bustled off to another room and returned with a Russian doll set. I saw at once why she thought the museum might be interested. It was very old. At a glance, I felt certain it was pre-war, but it was missing the largest doll. And whilst it rattled, I couldn't initially open the first doll up.'

'So, how do you know there was a note in there?'

Charlie drank deeply and smacked his lips. 'Patience. Anyway, she told me how much she wanted for it, and I could see why the museum had baulked. I asked her if she wanted to sell anything else, and she said that this was the only thing she was interested in getting rid of. It had a sad history and she wanted it out of her house.'

'Sad history?'

'Well, yes, that certainly attracted my attention, but she refused to say any more. By now we were on the vodka and I must have been mellowing, because lo-and-behold I went and paid her the full price! I wandered back to my hotel with the doll in a plastic bag, chiding myself as a fool for the little old lady routine. Anyway, I boxed it up and posted it home, and flew on to Baghdad.'

'Baghdad. They let you in?'

Charlie seemed peeved for a moment, and then remembered there was no point in acting indignant in front of Julius. They knew each other too well.

'Yes, now then, you see, that was a misunderstanding,' he said, and they both laughed. Julius was properly intrigued now.

'So, what happened when you got home?' he asked.

'Well, the central heating had done its standard job and had very gently dried the wood, and voila, it opened up. Inside were five more nested dolls. I opened each doll, lining up the whole set, and inside the final one, the size of a thumbnail, was a little folded note.' Charlie paused. 'Thirsty work, this.'

Julius grinned and headed to the bar. He had to wait as a bunch of students debated over the various merits of ale or lager. One of the girls stepped aside to let him stand at the bar beside her. As she smiled at him, he remembered he needed some more toothpaste. Getting their drinks, he hurried back to his friend.

'You are rubbish with girls, aren't you?' Julius looked at Charlie, puzzled. *What on earth was he on about?* Sometimes that was a clear failing in Charlie. Always off on a tangent.

'The note! What did the note say?'

Charlie rolled his eyes. At school, the other boys had marvelled at Julius' lack of self-awareness. A few subtle advances also ruled out his interest in boys as well. He just seemed utterly without desire. Unless it was an old book or a maths problem, he just didn't engage.

'Charlie. The note.'

'Now you're interested,' he teased, gesturing his pint towards the bar. 'Gorgeous girl, cracking figure? Nothing. Piece of paper in an old wooden toy? All ears. Okay,' he said, and raised his hands as Julius glared at him. 'So, the note. On it, written in Cyrillic, was the following message: "The family egg is in the first doll".'

'It's probably nothing,' said Julius.

'There's more. I called up the old lady, Zofia, and asked if she remembered where the outer doll was. She said her brother-in-law had it. The brothers had fallen out and their grandfather had said families should stick together. He gave Filip the outer doll and Jan the inner set. He sealed both of them and said the boys should bring them together and heal their rift. I asked if that was typical of him, but she said she had never met the old man. She did say he'd been a soldier during the Russian revolution!'

'Oh,' Julius said, and leant back in his chair crossing his arms. He looked up at the ceiling as he thought about it, a small, excited grin lighting up his face. It was simply impossible to not hear eggs, Russia and hidden clues without homing in like an Exocet on the inevitable conclusion.

A Fabergé egg.

Could it be that one of the famed missing imperial eggs was about to be found? Or at least that a genuine clue might have come to the surface. So many treasures of the Russian imperial court had been lost following the revolution. The jewelled Easter eggs made by Carl Fabergé for the Romanov royal family were the most sought out of them all.

The two men talked excitedly, guessing who the *family* might refer to, if indeed it even was a Fabergé that the note was referring to.

'So that's what I need from you,' announced Charlie. 'I don't know anyone better than you at research. Can you investigate our babushka's husband's grandfather? Everything you can find. Also, I need you to find the brother. But, you know, don't mention this to anyone. Not even, what was her name, Rebecca?'

Julius gulped. Rebecca! Checking his watch, he realised he was late. So much for not being distracted.

#3 Neith – Alpha Earth

Stepping through the Q Field was disconcerting. Until you became used to it, it usually resulted in vomiting, or screaming, or fluency in French or Mandarin. Some came through convinced they had tails that had failed to materialise. Others thought they were fish. Some never recovered and became gardeners. Some died. Although deaths were rare, the pre-vetting process was thorough. I liked to think of us as the best of the best. Others liked to think of us as unhinged psychopaths.

As I stepped onto the landing apron, Clio was standing to my left and we both stepped smartly away from the quantum field. A perfect transition. In the past, quantum curators would have been greeted with a round of applause, but these days that was considered showy. Personally, I liked showy. I looked up to the guys on the gantry, who flashed us a thumbs up. A couple of officers with guns stood at the other side of the room, and we smiled at them. It was always a good idea to let the people pointing guns at you know that all was well.

Then the glass doors opened, and medics walked in, giving us restorative jabs and broad-spectrum antibiotics. Excalibur may not have been the only thing we carried back with us. Finally, the archivists came forward and removed the sword.

We headed to the changing rooms, where Clio had to drag me away from the gloriously hot shower, before we went upstairs and away from the Q Zone to give our report.

The Q Zone consisted of the Q Field itself, which was, to all intents and purposes, a blank wall; the large empty room, or landing apron; and then the lower and upper gantry for the personnel, with changing rooms and an emergency triage station to the side. Due to the side effects of the Q Field, most other departments and offices were located further away. It used to be a lot smaller, but an accidental incursion by rhinos had changed that. They'd had to pretty much rebuild the entire room after a terrified rhino had gone on the rampage. Now the Q Field opened onto a large empty room with the technicians on overhead gantries.

As soon as we stepped into the corridor I breathed a sigh of relief. I loved the warm, dry Alexandrian climate and I couldn't wait to get outside and bathe in the warm air, maybe even take a quick swim in the Mareotis. Proper clean water. In the meantime, we discussed how we would approach the report.

'Which bit do you think we'll get bollocked the most for? Miscalculating the weight of the sword or not packing proper scuba gear?'

Clio thought about it. 'It's going to be the weight thing. The lack of full scuba gear didn't impact on the mission, and as it turned out we were able to successfully weave into one of the established Arthurian myths.'

I frowned. Both of us should have spotted the weight problem, but it was just the sort of thing that I was expected to overlook, forget about or miscalculate. Therefore, the onus of responsibility would fall unfairly on Clio's shoulders.

We headed into the chief's office, where the sword was already laid out on a preservation board. Once our report had been submitted, verified and approved, it would be attached to the board and then the two would be filed together in the vaults a few hundred metres beneath our feet, ready for further processing.

The Library of Alexandria was one facet of our mouseion complex, and I might be biased, but our mouseion was the best in the world given that it was home to all the unique and lost items from Beta Earth. There isn't a Beta comparison, as their *museums* are a pale shadow of the glories of a proper mouseion. Each branch was split into the nine muses, so we had the library department, the art department, the music department, the artefact department... Well, you get it. And all are currently being filled up with specimens from Beta Earth.

'Morning, ladies. Who wants to explain the cock-up then?'

Captain Samuel Nymens was responsible for the quantum curators. He was our first port of call when things went wrong, and our first line of defence when the higher-ups decided to chew us out for mistakes. He could tear into us, shout at us and kick our arses there and back again, but beyond this room, he would defend us to the hilt. A good guy to have on your side. Even when he was screaming in your face. Today, he seemed to be in a forgiving mood. I took a risk.

'My fault, sir. Clio asked me to collate the item specifics. I forgot to get the weight.'

Sam raised an eyebrow whilst Clio stood stock-still beside me. Stepping in now to contradict me would suggest a lack of team unity. Possibly a greater sin.

'Is that correct, Clio?'

'Sir?'

'Did Neith fail to log the weight of the sword?'

'Yes, sir.'

'That you asked her to do?'

'Sir?'

'Neith says you asked her to collate its dimensions.'

'Sir?'

'Well?'

'You haven't asked me a question, sir.'

'Did you, or did you not, ask Neith to calibrate the item's measurements?'

'Sir. Neith has already stated that to be the case.'

'What?'

'For me to suggest otherwise would suggest that Neith had lied.'

A pause lingered between the three of us. A lie would suggest a reckless operative and an inharmonious team dynamic. The fact that the three of us knew I was notorious for not quite telling the whole truth was being happily ignored. So long as the job got done, who cared? That was my attitude. Besides, better a minor rebuke on my report than on Clio's.

Sam's face twitched, causing his moustache to quiver, and then he sighed. 'Sit down and report.'

Clio gave her report as my eyes wandered around the room. Sam's office was lined with books, sporting memorabilia, and musical instruments. Any spare wall space featured works of art by his children. Doodles by them mastering the art of crayons or paint. Where there weren't works of art, there were photos of his family beaming out at him. They sure were a fine family. Sam was the very epitome of a good-looking man; tall and strong, with blue eyes and black hair. His skin was the colour of wet sand and his eyes sparkled. Even the crow's feet around his eyes seemed to highlight just how attractive they were. Blue eyes weren't uncommon here in northern Africa, but they were definitely in the minority. The rest of us just had to work our shades of brown. His children were all equally appealing, as was his wife. Sickeningly, they were all bloody lovely people as well.

'Neith! I said report.'

I jumped, then confirmed that Clio had given an accurate report, whatever she had just said. I went on to relate my side of the mission. Clio agreed that, as much as she was able to comment on that, it was an accurate assessment of the extraction.

'Right. Well done, ladies. A successful, if unusual retrieval.'

King of the understatement. Normally we recovered priceless works of art or lost masterpieces: Leonardo's lost notebooks, Mozart's symphonies, Rembrandt's sea paintings. All safely secured in our vaults. Every item was copied to the last detail in perfect holographic and 3D facsimile to be borrowed or studied by anyone on the planet. The original was safely cared for in the vaults, which again, anyone could visit. But why bother? We had made it as accessible as possible to the entire world.

The sword of some quasi-mythical warlord was not our normal fare. Certainly, it was talked about reverentially on Beta Earth, but not here on Alpha Earth. We had long since moved away from concepts of religion and warfare.

The theory was that our earth and their earth parted at the burning of the Library of Alexandria. At least that's what the philosophers and scientists suggest. They also postulate that if we have one parallel universe, we can have a myriad. There could be earths where the dinosaurs were never wiped out; there could be earths where mankind never got going; there could be earths where mankind had already become extinct; there could even be earths where putting milk in your tea first was acceptable. Who knew? I tended to fall asleep during these lectures. All we knew for certain was that there was our earth, and there was Beta Earth.

Back when the Romans had burnt the library, we responded differently to Beta Earth. The lands of northern Africa and Persia had banded together, and history had pivoted. That's pretty simplistic but it will do for now. The Roman Army was attacked continually until, starved of grain and undermined by politics, it collapsed. Octavius fell and drowned in the glorious Aegean after a rowdy party, and the Roman Empire failed to emerge.

From there, the Conclave of Mali agreed that nation-building was going to destroy us. Instead, we began to focus on sharing knowledge. Mouseions became the leading forces. Certainly, there were skirmishes between ruling deans and chancellors, but gradually we grew into a political structure based on knowledge and discovery. Without constant warfare for territorial rights, we worked on hunger and disease and an equitable division of population and resources. It was all perfect. Although, if I were honest and I said this to myself in perfect silence, it was incredibly dull.

I wasn't alone. On Beta Earth, I'd have been a soldier or an adventurer; words filled with concern or scorn over here. Instead, my sort became groundbreakers. We would help tame the land for new colonies of people heading out onto new continents. Working alongside the indigenous residents, we would manipulate the migration routes of buffalos or take out the odd tiger.

With Leonardo's discovery of the quantum field, my sort were the foolhardy idiots who threw themselves off into adventures unknown. Lack of warfare, famine or short life expectancies meant that scientific endeavours occurred quicker and worked better.

Don't get me wrong, Beta Earth is not without random moments of scientific brilliance, but without the proper infrastructure, they tended to explode and fizzle out. We'd had supersonic flight since the early 1800s. Beta Earth had it briefly and then it collapsed. Same with Portable Electricity Storage. They still haven't progressed past a battery that can power a child's toy.

Which is a roundabout way of me saying that we don't tend to value weapons of war, items that promised the resurrection of a nation's Golden Age or, worst of all, a religious artefact? Along with nation-building, religion had been given a stern talking to. If people wanted to believe in gods, then all well and good, but if it couldn't be proved then it wasn't to leave the front door.

As a culture, no one complained about the lack of executions, tortures, persecutions or deprivations.

Dismissed, the pair of us headed out, leaving Sam to ponder on why we were recovering swords. Clio punched me on the arm.

'Wally, you could've ended up on desk duty for the entire weekend.'

'Yeah, well, I didn't, and besides which, now you owe me. First round's on you!'

#4 Julius – Beta Earth

Julius dashed out of the pub; promising Charlie he would be back in touch the next day to see what his initial investigations had unearthed. He ran along the pavement, and as he pulled on the door to the wine bar, a group of women spilled out. There was some laughter and gentle mocking, and Julius realised he knew them. These were some of Rebecca's friends, and indeed, the last girl out of the door was Rebecca herself, who looked a lot less pleased to see him than her friends had.

'Nice of you to turn up.' She frowned as he leant forward to give her a peck on the cheek, then sniffed. 'Have you been drinking?'

'Just a quick beer with an old school friend.' He was going to suggest introducing her but paused. Rebecca was not likely to approve of Charlie.

'Have you been waiting long? I'm so sorry. Text me next time?'

'Check your phone!'

Julius checked his phone and saw various missed calls and texts, all from Rebecca, and found his phone in silent mode.

'Oops, sorry, my phone was switched to silent.'

'Well, of course it was. I didn't think you were ignoring me.'

Rebecca enjoyed the prestige of having such a good-looking companion, but honestly, she wasn't sure if he was worth the effort. He could be interminably boring and never once paid her a compliment. On an early date, she had pressed him to say something nice about her. He told her that her hair was clean. She stopped fishing for compliments after that. They had been dating for about two months but just didn't seem to be getting anywhere. Having a boyfriend worth showing off only went so far.

'Shall we go in?' Julius asked.

Rebecca's friends had stepped to one side and were waiting a few yards off, but Julius and Rebecca were still standing in front of the door.

'Go in?' Rebecca looked confused, and Julius gestured towards the pub.

'Oh no. Not now. I bumped into some of the girls whilst I was waiting for you and they're off to the cinema. I said I'd go with them.'

'Oh. Right. What's the film?'

'*Waiting to Love You.*'

'Isn't that the one we saw last weekend?'

'Yes. And now I'm going to see it again.'

It seemed odd to Julius to go and watch a boring film twice, but he never quite understood Rebecca. She always seemed to be unhappy, or annoyed, or out and out cross in his company. He wasn't even sure why they were going out, but he didn't want to be rude and ask. Anyway, now he was free to get back to the library and carry on with the Romanovs. Already distracted by the paper chase, he gave her a quick kiss on the top of her head, told her he hoped she'd have a fun time, then strode off back to the library.

Rebecca stood in front of the door looking vexed. In her scenario, he was going to lavishly apologise and plead with her to let him make it up to her. She'd turn to her friends with a *What can you do?* smile and be the envy of them all. Now, as she turned to them, she was convinced Helen was smirking. Clare was downright concerned, chiding her for being mad. She knew the girls thought she should work harder to keep him interested, but honestly, they had no idea how tiresome the absent-minded genius routine became after a few days. She didn't approve at all.

Julius pushed back from his terminal. It was three am and he needed to sleep. Priming the small library's alarm system, he locked up and walked home. The streets were mostly empty, bar a few stragglers from the pubs and nightclubs. The only other signs of life were the huddled forms sleeping in doorways or alleyways. Occasionally a taxi drove past, but Julius wanted the fresh air to process his thoughts.

As a professor and a long-time bona fide researcher at the museum, Julius had access to an enormous range of academic and government sources. Most were fairly pedestrian, but a while ago he had earned himself a higher security clearance level, and he could now view classified files, including an info dump of KGB and Politburo figures.

A few years earlier, Julius had been looking at details of a Russian train timetable. It wasn't a classified document, just tedious, and Julius had offered to help out a colleague who was writing a paper on Soviet coal production. There was a note in the margin explaining a five-minute delay in departure. The delay was apparently due to Stalin having to wait for someone to board the train. This intrigued Julius and he started to poke around until he discovered that, according to official records, Stalin had been in Moscow all day.

Julius sent that little revelation to the Home Office, who instantly made the file classified whilst they investigated what Stalin might have been up to. They also upped Julius' clearance level. Her Majesty's Government always liked a sharp pair of eyes. So long as those eyes were on their side. The British Government had a difficult relationship with Cambridge scholars, especially in all matters pertaining to Russia. However, they had vetted Julius to within an inch of his life and found nothing untoward, so now he got to rummage around lots of interesting case files.

Which was just as well, because here he was leafing through Russian military documents. In and of themselves, they were pretty boring; what the British Government had was mostly redacted, or at least that which Julius was allowed to read. His clearance level only went so far. Some of the documents the cold war spies had smuggled out of Russia were incendiary, others were plebeian. But plebeian was what Julius needed. So many times, massive secrets were discovered behind mundane facts and figures. Now Julius thought about what he had unearthed as the cold wind whipped off the Cambridge fens.

The old woman's grandfather-in-law was called Dimitri Guskov. He had indeed been stationed in Moscow, and then for a brief stint was registered as being at the Ipatiev House, Yekaterinburg. There were no details of his duties, but what else was there to do there in 1918, other than guard the soon to be assassinated imperial family?

Dimitri then married and had a son. His son moved to Poland and went on to have two sons himself, Filip and Jan. Jan married Zofia and they bought a flat in Warsaw. This was Charlie's babushka. This was as far as Julius had got. Zofia's brother-in-law was harder to find. Julius had unearthed a wedding announcement and a photo of Jan and Zofia, but there was no mention of Filip, or even that Jan had a brother. Could this indicate a death? Maybe a rift?

Julius had begun to track the brother down. So far he hadn't found a death certificate, but he also hadn't found any other details. Tomorrow he would investigate the emigration records.

#5 Neith – Alpha Earth

Great Ra! Why did I drink last night? A Q hangover was nothing like a regular one. Drinking after a Q Step was always tricky, and normally I avoided it, but I'd been so annoyed at my stupidity that I was in the mood to live it up. Adding alcohol to a brain that had only just processed a shift in quantum states was particularly foolhardy.

Clio had suggested we go let our hair down at one of the chess clubs, but the last time I was there everyone had got really cross with me. In fairness, there are some tables you probably shouldn't dance on. So, we'd gone to Pygs instead. Pygs was a place favoured by the underbelly of society, the roughnecks and rule breakers, the quantum librarians and curators. Basically, it was where I was most at home. But dear Anubis, this morning's headache was severe and at one point I found myself conversing in twelfth-century Cantonese. I felt shivery and the light was killing my eyes.

Holding onto my coffee cup for dear life, I pulled my coat closer, put on my sunglasses and slid into the briefing room. I was instantly met with a barrage of hoots and cat-calls. Yeah, like none of them had ever suffered a little step death.

Gingerly, I removed my sunnies and waved to everyone, acknowledging the jeers. We were nothing if not a team, and I knew I'd be hooting with laughter just as loudly if any of them arrived at a meeting so clearly suffering. Some people show their love with flowers and chocolates, we sent punches and piss-takes. I slumped down into a chair next to Ramin.

'When did you get back?'

'Yesterday.'

'And you went for a drink straight away? Man, do you even have a brain?'

I groaned. 'Not currently. Currently, I have a brass band rioting in my head. I assume that the polar bear over there's a hallucination?'

Ramin didn't bother looking where I was pointing. If there had been a polar bear here in Egypt, it would be attracting a little more attention than just mine.

I tried to focus on my fingers and watched as the fish leapt from nail to nail. At least I knew these weren't a figment of my imagination. Last night in the bar, Clio had been painting my nails. She was a genius at the micro subroutines embedded in the varnish; right now, little goldfish were launching out of blue-green polish, surrounded by little lily pads, and then splashing into the water of the next nail. She even had the little hologram creating ripples and splashes in the varnish. Like I said, an artist. Quantum curators, or steppers, as we tended to call ourselves, couldn't have tattoos for obvious reasons, so instead, we played with holograms that could be removed and deactivated as we stepped across into the historically-sensitive time period.

Painting holograms also calmed her down. When we'd walked into the bar, Tyler started jeering at me for having to pretend to be the Lady of the Lake. What can I say? Tyler's a camel's arse, always has been, always will be. Not worth the spit. But if Clio has an Achille's heel, it's those she cares for.

One time in basic training, she was unhappy with how a fellow student had referred to Clio's favourite teacher. The student in question was a huge bloke, well over six foot. Clio knocked him out cold. The only reason she wasn't put on remand was because he categorically refused to acknowledge she had decked him. For the next few weeks, that teacher received loads of gifts from fellow students. All of them made sure Clio knew it was them who had given a gift.

So, of course, Tyler kicking off was just the sort of thing to bug Clio; she was a tad overprotective and able to start a fight in an empty room. And win. All I wanted was a fun night, lots of laughs and a drink or two. So first I braided her hair, so I could literally hold her down, and then I got her to do my nails. And then we laughed, and I drank too much.

I groaned again as the fish subroutine started again, and rested my head on Ramin's shoulder.

'Wally,' he said. Throwing his arm around my shoulder, he gave me a hug then handed me an energy tab. It would be my tenth this morning. One of them had to work, surely?

Sitting next to Ramin was Paul. They had stepped back from their mission that morning, otherwise, they'd have been out with us the night before. Which could have been a blessing or a curse. Ramin would have convinced me to stick to tomato juice, Paul would have challenged me to a shots race, and we'd both be waking up in casualty. Again.

He leaned past Ramin and knuckled me on the head. 'Morning gorgeous! You and Clio up for lunch after briefing?'

Trying not to vomit, I weakly agreed, wondering when this torture would pass. Ramin gave me another tab and grinned at me as I tried not to fall asleep, or pass out. If Clio was my best friend, Ramin was like my brother. We'd been mates since childhood when I first arrived in playgroup wearing feathers in my hair. All the other children had looked at me weirdly. The following day, Ramin came in wearing feathers as well. We had been inseparable since then. Then there was Paul, and if Clio was my best friend and Ramin was my soulmate, then Paul was great in the sack. We'd been dating on and off since he moved to this division. We competed in everything and cheered each other on. Life was uncomplicated and enjoyable. Occasionally we'd been asked if we were going to move to a more official setting, but who needed the hassle? Life was good. Why spoil it?

Clio dashed in ahead of the bosses and handed me some water. Great Ra, I loved that girl.

A general wave of silence permeated the room as Chancellor Soliman Alvarez walked in. The chancellor's presence was unusual at a weekly briefing, and we became a little more alert. In his normal pompous manner, he welcomed us and asked Sam to bring the room up to date with the previous week's recoveries. Some were mundane. A poem, a speech never given, a painting never shown. Others were flashier, like Shakespeare's copy of *Love's Labour's Won*.

The problem was how the quantum field worked. When we stepped through, we wore a wrist brace that was effectively tethered to the Q Field. When it was time to come home, we would hit recall and we'd be pulled back. Because the quantum bungee cord was always there, the technicians could also snap us back if we were late or ill. But not if we were dead. It seemed that the Q Field recognised the lack of brain waves, and spontaneously cut the cord.

The science on how it interacted with brain waves wasn't fully understood yet, but we did know that it only seemed to be human brain waves. We'd tried placing a quantum harness on an animal, but the Q Field couldn't tell where the animal ended and the harness began, and sometimes it fused them.

After a while, new protocols had to be imposed. It was simply too distressing for all involved. For a while, very brave souls stepped through holding or leading the animals. Once again, the Q Field failed to properly differentiate the two life forms. The resulting chimeric messes were considered too high a risk to continue to bring through livestock. Although we did have an incredible drill instructor in training, who had fabulous wings and a beaked face. We all called her Horus, although not in front of her. And after Clio's little outburst, the nickname died altogether.

'And of course, yesterday Neith became the Lady of the Lake.'

The hoots and laughter started up again. Oh, the embarrassment to be caught playing a mythical character. Especially with the chancellor in the room. One of the things that had allowed our earth to flourish and grow was a lack of religious systems. Some semi-religious belief systems existed, but they didn't extend beyond, "be nice to people and take care of things". It was a philosophy that pretty much all of us respected and understood. Sam continued to explain about the recovery of the sword, which led to a few puzzled glances. He then continued to outline the briefing for the week ahead.

'Hang on,' I said and nudged Ramin, 'what about your retrieval?'

Ramin frowned and said he'd tell me about it later. In the meantime, Sam was wrapping up. 'Finally, ladies and gentlemen, we possibly have a live event currently unfolding.'

Everyone, including me, sat up.

#6 Julius – Beta Earth

'I've found him!' Julius was so excited that he had almost fumbled the phone as he dialled Charlie's number. He loved a treasure hunt and he had been chasing Filip Guskov all across Europe. Every time Julius had found Filip's name on a legal document, he moved again. Eventually, he appeared to be living in London, having changed his name to Philip Guscott.

Filip—or Philip—had worked in the publishing trade and had finally retired to a house in London he had bought in the 1980s, just before the market had exploded. He had modified his name slightly to sound more British, and it was that which had made the paper trail go cold. Lots of Polish and German emigres altered their names in the fifties. For whatever reason, they wanted to blend in. Some had a survivor's fear of never wishing to stand out, whilst others wanted to blend into the background for entirely opposite reasons.

At the other end of the phone, Charlie told Julius to slow down while he grabbed a pen and notepad. 'Shoot, and please don't give me the location of a cemetery.'

Julius laughed. 'No, as far as I can tell he's alive and kicking and of relatively sound mind and body. He's a retired publisher, still writes the occasional column for various magazines, and is the branch secretary for a local bird spotting group. According to their Facebook page, he regularly walks a few miles along the Thames Valley towpath.'

'The Thames! You mean—'

'Yep. Right here in good old Blighty. You can put your passport away.'

'Okay, so you've found the estranged brother. Now, tell me about the grandfather. In your opinion, am I on a wild goose chase?'

'Right, so Zofia's grandfather-in-law, if that's the right term, was called Dimitri Guskov and he was a Russian soldier during the revolution.' Julius paused to drink his coffee and Charlie cut in.

'Damn, is that it? I was hoping you might have been able to find out a bit more.'

'If you'll let me finish. I did find more. After he left the army he married a German girl and moved west. They had two sons, and the rest you know.'

'So, that's it then?'

Julius grinned to himself. 'Well, there is one other little fact I dug up. Guskov was stationed at Ipatiev House in 1918. But listen, there's something else...' Julius smiled as Charlie whistled down the phone.

Ipatiev House was etched in blood. Tsar Nicolas II, his wife Tsarina Alexandra and their five children, ranging in age from twenty-two to thirteen, were assassinated in a cold, damp basement room. It was an act that sent shock waves across Europe. Charlie was even more determined now to go and visit Dimitri Guskov's grandson. Could he be on the path of an uncovered Fabergé egg? The temptation to keep it was high; what a thing to own. However, it was nowhere near as tempting as netting a quick twenty million or more. God knows, as yet he had no idea which egg it was. It might not even be an imperial egg. It might not even be a Fabergé. He had to try to remain calm and focussed. The grandson might not even have the other doll casing anymore. But what if he did? What if he had never opened his grandfather's seal? What if an egg was hidden inside after all those years?

Rebecca looked up at Julius. He was trying very hard to make up for last week's lapse of judgement and had met her for lunch, presenting her with a lovely bunch of flowers. She wondered if he had an account somewhere, as he regularly gave her flowers to apologise for this or that. She wasn't complaining, but it might be nice if the flowers were just flowers, not apologies. He was now telling her enthusiastically about a set of auction catalogues he was currently going through, from a northern market town in the 1930s. Apparently, stuff like this was invaluable in tracking down provenance for various works of art. He had also been able to marry up some items with a banking ledger that had been catalogued a few years earlier.

'It's like finding a missing link. It might mean the discovery of a hidden masterpiece or the validation that granny's pretty vase is going to pay for her nursing. Stuff like this is incredible.'

She knew she wasn't as clever as Julius, not even close, but she wished occasionally he would find her fascinating. They had met at a quiz night where her team was smashing it. At the bar, he had smiled at her and said he and his team needed her expertise. Apparently, he didn't even watch TV. She had thought that was incredibly endearing. She didn't normally make the first move but had suggested that they go out for a drink and had been delighted by his surprised smile.

Now she tried to stifle a yawn. Whatever Julius was working on was always amazing or incredible. A new type of mediaeval hinge, amazing; a recipe for cheese, incredible; a diary entry for the yield of a field, revelatory. It didn't matter what the subject matter was or the time period, Julius found it all fascinating. Rebecca yawned again and made a point of looking around the room.

Julius grimaced. He had been playing back yesterday's conversation with Charlie in his head. The police report had said the death was unsuspicious, but Julius was alarmed. Charlie, however, wasn't. Old people died all the time; that was sort of the point. Even so, the discovery sat uncomfortably with Julius, who hoped his friend was not getting involved in something dangerous. Just as he was about to replay the conversation again, he noticed Rebecca was yawning.

He knew he was rubbish with girls. They were clearly worth the effort, he just wished he were better at it. He thought Rebecca was a lovely girl who always saw the world differently, in a way that was refreshing to him, but he didn't seem to be able to convey that. He had tried once to explain how he felt about her and was horrified when she asked if she was some sort of experiment. He knew she was upset, but he wasn't sure how he had hurt her and tried harder to be attentive. The problem was, he was no good at small talk; he didn't tend to notice current affairs or the weather, he rarely watched TV or read the papers, and probably couldn't pick the current prime minister out of a line-up, let alone which party they represented. Talking about his work seemed to constantly bore her, so he moved to a subject that he was sure would please her. 'How's your day been?'

Rebecca's attention swung back to him and, stabbing a broccoli stalk, she waved it at him. 'You remember Nikki? You'll never guess what she did in the new window display.'

Julius nodded appreciatively as Rebecca launched into a tale of high skulduggery in the Jonas Dept Display Team. Rebecca was a display designer for the department store, displaying goods to their most enticing best and guaranteeing sales. Apparently, Nikki had positioned one of the mannequins in the window so that it appeared to be pinching another mannequin's bottom. Julius duly laughed and then apologised as Rebecca explained to him that it wasn't actually funny.

'It's like she doesn't take her job seriously. We have standards, you know.'

At this Julius could sympathise. He knew Rebecca worked hard and was proud of all she had achieved. Her thematic windows often made the local papers, and she had made the new season window reveals into something of an event. Last Christmas the police had to temporarily close the street as the crowd was so large. Julius knew she was looking for a promotion. She deserved it, but her company were quite traditional. They wouldn't create a new position for her, so she was likely going to have to move. Julius knew she had London firmly in her sights.

'That reminds me. I was talking to Charlie today.'

Rebecca stared at him blankly. She had been discussing the new layout of the perfume floor and what Gino had said to her about customer targeting. Had Julius been listening to a word she said?

Returning to his college office after lunch, he tried to concentrate on his paper on the Myth and Migration Patterns of the Early Hallstatt Cultures, but he couldn't focus. No matter how much he tried to settle down, his mind drifted to his earlier conversation. Charlie had asked if he wanted to accompany him to visit Zofia's elusive brother-in-law. Julius knew this was a big deal. If Charlie was on the path of a Fabergé, then it showed great faith and trust that he had invited him along. He had almost said yes, it was that tempting. Then he thought about all the effort involved and decided he preferred his treasure hunts in the old library stacks and the pages of the web. All within reach of a decent cup of coffee or a warming glass of single malt. What was the appeal of getting cold and wet, running down leads in the rain, hanging around in strange places and wondering when you'd be back in your own bed? Both his best friend and his girlfriend were outward going sorts. Maybe he should try a little harder. He knew Charlie understood him. Maybe if Julius tried a bit harder with Rebecca she'd understand him as well.

#7 Neith – Alpha Earth

Live events were treasured. You could play fast and loose with the timeline as there was less to screw up. They were also high risk, with a greater chance of failure or death, and a greater chance of glory. No wonder we were all leaning forward in our seats. The Q Field was capable of letting us through to any place on Beta Earth in any time zone, but sometimes it lined up with Beta Earth at the same time we were currently at, hence a live event.

'It looks like a Fabergé egg is about to resurface.' Clio nudged me, and the flush of adrenaline through my system swept away the hangover. Just like that, the polar bear disappeared and all I had was a slight mussiness. The joy of quantum hangovers. I pushed my sunglasses up onto my head to get a better view of the large screen behind Captain Nymens.

According to record, Carl Fabergé made only fifty eggs for the royal imperial family of Russia. The locations of forty-four were known to Beta Earth. We knew of a further two that were in undeclared private collections, and another two were in our own vaults. That left a further two whose locations were truly unknown. It would be our job to watch the path of its discovery. We would monitor it right until the moment it went public or was melted down.

Believe me, that nearly happened once.

We had been getting ready to grab the egg. Someone had bought it at a flea market and didn't realise what it was. Idiot. Anyway, he could see it was made of gold and jewels and thought he would melt it down and sell it for scrap. However, the surprise that this egg contained was a watch, and the bloke thought he might be able to flog it. He did a quick internet search for the watch, and mentioned the egg as well, and suddenly he was receiving lots of search results about missing Fabergé eggs. Needless to say, he didn't melt the egg down after that.

If it hadn't been saved though, we would have stepped in. At the moment that the item is destroyed, we are then able to enact the live protocol. The Q Field confirming the item has left the Beta timeline permanently then opens a window for us to step through. We head back a few days or weeks beforehand and prepare to extract it at the moment of destruction.

'Any questions?'

There was a sea of hands. This was going to be a hotly contested assignment.

'Which egg is it? Have we got any intel yet?'

'No, nothing yet.'

'Do we know which continent it's on?'

'All the intel suggests Europe at the moment. Or Asia,'

There were lots of groans. Researching two continents was twice the workload. At least it was a Fabergé. That meant only a hundred years of research.

'Any sense of timescale?'

'Not yet. The quantum alert has only thrown this up as a possibility at this moment. As we get closer to the event, we'll get more details. And no, we don't have any names yet either.'

Which meant loads of tedious fact-finding about stuff that we would ultimately need to ditch. Step forward, Clio. I was okay at research and loved tracking down active clues, but Clio was a beast at it. It was a toss-up between her and Ramin as to who was better.

'Any idea what the hidden treasure is, or if it's present?'

I watched as Sam raised an eyebrow at Tyler. It was a stupid question and he had almost certainly ruled himself and his partner, off the team. Every egg had been crafted to contain a unique treasure. When the jewelled egg was open, something special was hidden inside. A portrait, an automaton, a jewel, a toy; all in miniature. No two were the same.

'If we knew what the treasure was, Curator Jones, then we'd know what the egg was, wouldn't we?' asked the chancellor in an openly mocking tone. 'I think you need to spend a bit more time in the library and not the gym. Yes?'

I looked at Sam's impassive face. As captain, it was his place to comment and discipline his curators, but the chancellor outranked him. Still, it was an unnecessary rudeness both to Sam and Tyler. Not that I cared much for Tyler.

Ignoring the interruption Sam cleared his throat and dismissed the room, reminding all of us that an hour in the gym was as important as an hour in the library and that neither should be neglected.

As we left, Tyler barged past us, and the four of us headed out into the sunshine and down to Snaps, our favourite riverbank bar. There was always a lovely breeze at this time of day, and they served a mean melon slushie.

We pulled up our chairs and relaxed in the shade. Out on the river a few teenagers were playing on the hover punts, trying to goad the crocodiles for a bit of sport, but these crocs were old and sleepy and used to the irritations of children. Occasionally, one would snap its jaw, causing the kids to scream with laughter, and their mothers to come down to the edge to admonish their children. It was mean to torment the crocodiles; even if they fell off their boards, their exo-suits would bubble up and protect them from drowning, or falling, or being bitten in half, or any one of the myriad ways in which children tried to kill themselves.

I remember playing with the crocs as a child, but when we did it Ramin and I both switched off our exo-suits. Where was the fun if there was no risk? Shortly after that, we'd been reassigned schools to a place more suitable to our skills and attitudes. The Library of Alexandria.

'So, an egg!'

Paul looked as excited as I felt. The last egg hunt had involved an exploding tanker, and the one before that had taken part during the fall of the Berlin Wall. Fun times.

'Which teams do you reckon they'll pick?' We were both in with a chance. No one could step within seven days of their last step; it was a simple safety protocol and for the next week, none of us could be considered, but on day eight we'd be eligible. So long as we weren't then assigned to another retrieval. We discussed it for a while, all agreeing that we hoped the Fabergé Event spun out slowly. It would be just our luck if it sped up.

Clio sipped on a cucumber smoothie and asked the boys why there had been no mention of their mission in the weekly briefing.

They looked at each other and shrugged. 'We've been instructed not to discuss it with anyone.'

We both smiled at them, our eyebrows raised in matching expressions.

'Yeah, okay, fair enough.'

They looked at each other and nodded. 'It's not like we weren't going to talk to you about it.'

'Yeah, I mean Sam practically said "Talk to no one about this. Except Neith and Clio".'

'Yeah. I mean, he didn't say the bit about you two out loud.'

'No, not out loud as such, but yeah, reading between the lines.'

'Exactly, Sam could hardly expect us not to talk to you two about it.'

This was interesting. Clio sat forward. 'So, what happened?'

'We were stepping over to pick up Rembrandt's *The Storm on the Sea of Galilee.*'

'Oh ho, you got that one? Was it a total nightmare?'

The Q Field had a programmed list of lost items from Beta Earth that were available to claim. It was a long list, and it would randomly generate the next lost treasure to go and track down. There were generally three or four a week, sometimes as many as ten. It could be a painting, a book, even a plant. There was no rhyme or reason, but when the stars aligned, we were to go and grab it. Honestly, I suspect it's more complicated than when the stars align, and I know we had to study it for five years in high school. Ultimately, the most I understood, I mean really understood, was that when we were told to jump, we stepped.

Rembrandt's seascape was one of the larger items on the list. It had been stolen in a raid on the Gardner Museum over fifty years before, along with a collection of other works of art. Most were in private collections, but the Rembrandt was so large that the thieves had been unable to fence it quickly and storage had been an issue, so they burnt it. Philistines.

A quantum slot had opened up and a team were tasked to go back and grab it before it was burnt. These sorts of extractions were always tricky, as you had to ensure that the involved parties—the idiots burning the art—couldn't know that the painting hadn't actually burnt. We had a range of tactics to ensure the timeline remained stable. Early attempts of "Shh, don't tell anyone" failed massively and prompted a slew of alien visitation reports on Beta Earth. It was all a bit embarrassing. Now we relied on sleight of hand, auto-suggestion, and good old drugs. *The Storm on the Sea of Galilee* was almost two metres tall. That was going to require some manipulation. Plus, a fire was always tricky to fake.

'What did you go with, drugs or a dummy? Don't tell me it did get burnt?' asked a horrified Clio.

It did happen. Despite our best efforts, we occasionally failed to save the item and we had to step back empty handed and wait for the next quantum window to open up, which could be the next week or a decade later. It was the sort of error that first years made, not seasoned steppers like Paul and Ramin.

'No, nothing that mundane. When we arrived on Beta Earth we started to investigate the brief. Imagine our surprise when we saw the painting in pride of place in the National Museum of Art.'

'What!?' It was hard to say which of us sounded more astounded.

'What the hell? Was it a fake?'

Ramin shook his head. 'No, we ran a full-spectrum analysis and it was the genuine article.'

'I don't understand. Had you arrived too early?'

'No. It'd been recovered the day before, and to great acclaim.'

'The thieves?'

'No, their identity remained unknown. The picture had been found propped up against a dumpster.'

'Was that on fire?'

'There was no fire.'

'So, what did you do?'

'Well, what could we do? We took a load of notes and then requested a step back.'

'Has that happened before? Anyone?'

We all shrugged. It was possible to arrive way before the extraction point or the day after. But arriving on time to find that the artefact was safe and sound? Unheard of. But had it happened before? Was the timeline not as secure as we thought it was?

'Do you want to know what the really weird bit is?' asked Ramin. 'When I left the debrief this morning, I checked the library catalogue and the picture's status. It's listed as Retrieved. According to the library, it did burn, and it was recovered. But when I pulled up the catalogue number, it showed an error report.'

Paul frowned at Ramin. 'What did you do that for? Sam could've put you on report and then you'd have lost any chance of going after this egg.'

Still, what Ramin had discovered was unsettling. 'That's pretty serious. What did Sam say?'

'I didn't mention it to him. Remember he'd told us to leave it alone.'

I continued to sip on my slushie. We worked for the library and tended not to ask questions. It was a fabulous job, working for a great organisation. The pay was good, and my colleagues were fun, so why would I question anything? And yet, that was two odd events in a row. A quasi-religious or mythical artefact retrieved, and a painting unburnt. And now we had a live event looming. What could go wrong?

8 Julius – Beta Earth

He knew his part in the hunt was done, but Julius couldn't let it go. When it came to dangling threads, he was like a terrier. Besides which, before he had only a basic awareness of Fabergé. Now he wanted to know more. Was it possible for him to guess which egg Charlie was on the trail of? Might knowing which one it was help him?

He could tackle this problem from two sides, what he knew about the current trail and what the world knew about the eggs. In his experience, you never tackled a problem from one angle only. You always tackled what was known and what was unknown. And whenever possible, you always started with primary sources. Which were not books, or websites or newspaper articles, but people.

Smiling, he dialled a number then headed out across Cambridge to Magdalene College to visit Marsha Favilova, a professor in cultural anthropology. The low morning sun was in his eyes, so he nipped through the alleys until he arrived at one of the side entrances. Showing his university ID to the porter, he headed into a small quadrangle. In summer this was one of his favourite gardens. The honeysuckle and roses filled the air with perfume as the red brick walls radiated warmth. Today though, the walls were bare except for the skeleton branches of the climbing shrubs. It had been so cold the night before that even in this sheltered garden, frost clung to the vines. Heading along the stone-flagged path, he entered the college and took the steps two at a time before knocking on Marsha's door. He loved visits to Marsha, even if they were always a bit full-on. Maybe because they were.

The door was flung open and a tall woman looked at him in horror.

'Julius. My boy! The cold! Do not stand there letting all the heat out. Come in, come in.'

As she closed the door, she looked as though he might have been in some way responsible for the cold, but that she would also be prepared to forgive him. She was almost as tall as Julius and was draped in a long, slim, black wool dress and covered in many layers of shawls, each artfully arranged and fixed by elaborate brooches. Several necklaces hung at her neck.

Kissing him on both cheeks she then took his face in her hands, looking at him sorrowfully.

'Ah, Julius. You are still so beautiful. There is so much sorrow for those so beautiful. It is a curse. Thank God I was not cursed with such beauty.'

Julius grinned at her. This bizarre ritual was well known to him. He had to find a way to tell her that she was beautiful, but that she would never know sorrow.

'You children. You think to offer compliments when you tell a woman she is beautiful,' she said, and sighed dramatically, 'but your heart is kind and I will accept and forgive your foolishness. In truth, your life will be long and painful, so it is my Christian duty to support you through your misery.'

This was one of the reasons why he loved Marsha; she was just so incredibly expressive. Everything was the end of the world. She appeared to be living in an era of Stalinist purges. Doom lay beyond every doorway, and she revelled in it.

'My misery might be assuaged by some of those spiced cakes you sometimes have around?'

Her lips twitched. 'You mock me, but that is good. You are young and full of life. Come in and sit down, then tell me what you need.'

Julius made himself comfortable. He reckoned Marsha was only about twenty years older than him, but in the winter she tended to go into old crone mode. In summer, she could be seen dancing with her undergrads out by the Cam. He didn't know if it was all an act or if this was genuine, but he honestly didn't care; she was refreshing, served a perfect cup of tea, and had a razor-sharp mind. Today he was here for her mind.

'I need to pick your brains about matryoshka dolls.'

'Cakes and dolls. What a lovely way to start the day. Excellent. What do you need to know?'

Julius explained that he was trying to track down the lost casing of an outer doll. He hadn't seen the inner dolls and had only had them described to him. All he hoped for was an idea of the size of the outer casing and maybe the subject matter.

They were seated in two comfortable armchairs and had a coffee table between them. Now Marsha wandered around her rooms, returning with doll sets until the table was covered in them.

'Okay. Matryoshka or Russian dolls are a nested set of wooden canisters. Each canister opens at the middle, revealing a smaller unit within. These reduce in size until you get to the smallest solid doll in the centre. You can have any number, but the preference is for around five or seven. The cluster of dolls is also thematic. Family members, politicians, et cetera. The inner doll is the smallest or least important, the outer doll is the most important. Another cake?'

Julius leant forward gratefully and, having put the cake on his plate, picked up one of the doll sets. Opening up the first doll, he looked inside.

'That set you're holding has a political theme. It's quite a modern set and made for the tourist market. Russians are more careful about political statements. Unless the statement is, "We support our current leader". In Russia, you know, we are famous for our freedom of speech. But those freedoms only last as long as the speech itself. I have a joke that will help you understand.'

Marsha cleared her throat. 'A frightened man came to the KGB. "My talking parrot has disappeared", she said in a gruff voice and then changed her pitch to reply as the KGB officer.

'That's not the kind of case we handle. Go to the criminal police.

'Excuse me, of course, I know that I must go to them. I am here just to tell you officially that I disagree with the parrot.'

Marsha laughed and slapped her leg. 'See! We are not idiots. Russian politics is for tourists.'

Julius laughed along with her as he stacked the dolls back together, his attention now taken with something more folk-like.

Marsha pointed to the old, faded doll he was holding. 'Now that one is the oldest in my collection and sounds like your doll. You see she is not as garish as these two?' said Marsha, pointing to two very pretty and slightly gaudy dolls. 'This one represents the seasons, that one is supposed to represent a traditional doll, but look at the two of them side by side.'

Julius looked at the modern doll, painted in a bright and traditional style. The face of the doll was blank and characterless. The older doll, however, was completely different. The paint was probably never quite so lurid, but more importantly, the face on the doll was realistic. This was a portrait. Julius felt certain that if he met the person in the flesh, he would recognise her. He opened the whole doll set and could see a family resemblance running through the dolls, from the outer matriarch to the little girl.

'Would an old one always be a woman on the outer casing?'

Marsha thought about it. 'I have seen male ones, but they were called *matryoshka* for a reason. If your outer casing is male and old, it would be quite collectable. However, you will be able to tell if it matches your set because the artistry between the dolls will be by the same hand. The inner dolls you have described sound as though they were not Soviet mass-produced items.'

The pair chatted on until a clock chimed and Marsha apologised, saying that she needed to go and teach. I have to work so that they will pay me. It's not like in the good old days when workers pretended to work, and bosses pretended to pay them. But this is progress!'

Kissing her on the cheeks, he set off. He had taken lots of measurements of her old dolls and now had an idea of the size of an outer doll, what it looked like and, given its thin wooden construction, the sort of volume it could hold. Which was basically not much more than the size of the next doll. These dolls had only a few millimetres between each layer, and would only lightly rattle rather than properly shake.

Now he needed to go and see which missing eggs might fit into an eight-inch case. Given that he didn't want to flag any interest levels on Fabergé eggs, he decided to hit the books and headed off to the main college library. It was a perfect example of industrial architecture, with its giant central tower dominating the surrounding landscape. It was not subtle, nor in Julius' mind particularly inviting. Its very presence issued a challenge to all who entered. Still, it was the largest library with the best general collection, and what he needed right now was a comprehensive oversight.

The first thing he discovered was how small the eggs were. It was entirely possible for most of them to fit within a matryoshka doll. The Easter eggs had been originally presented by the Tsar to his wife, and when he died, his son, Tsar Nicolas II continued the tradition but upped the ante. He presented an egg to his wife but also one to his mother; showing that for all his many, many faults he was a good boy that loved his mother. They were made of the finest materials and all of them contained a hidden surprise. Given the level of their artistry and the hidden treasure within them, Julius had assumed they would need to be much larger. Those hidden portraits, singing mechanical birds and clockwork trains must all be miniatures and all working perfectly. The artistry was breathtaking.

Fabergé didn't just make jewelled Easter eggs for the imperial family, but given that the potential provenance of Charlie's egg came from Dimitri Guskov, one of the Russian soldiers guarding the royal family in 1918, Julius decided to focus on the imperial eggs first.

Fifty were made, although a further two were under commission when the family were assassinated. Julius was intrigued by these two but decided that even if they did exist, Fabergé wouldn't have been able to get them to the family. So, back to fifty. The whereabouts of six eggs were currently unknown. However, the more he drilled down, the more he was able to narrow his search.

The location of two of them had been recorded during the mid-twentieth century. If the idea was that Charlie's egg had been hiding in a doll all these years, then it must have been missing almost from the beginning.

Only four fit this description, having been last itemised in 1922 at the Kremlin. Could the record have been falsified? Could one have been stolen after the inventory had been taken?

Can you steal something that was already stolen? When the imperial family had been assassinated, they had been told they were being moved to a safe location. Apparently, the tsarina and her five daughters lined their clothing with jewels and money. It took over ten minutes to kill them. Shots sprayed wildly as bullets ricocheted off all the diamonds and hidden treasures. No doubt as their bodies were taken to the carts, soldiers plundered the skirts and jackets, looting the precious gems. Had a little egg been hiding in a pocket?

Julius thought it very likely that treasure had been looted, but then how would you explain those four eggs turning up four years later on an inventory? Unless... Was it possible? Was there an unknown imperial egg? And if so, all bets were off as to its actual value.

#9 Neith – Alpha Earth

'Case FE 988776 is now active. Quantum Curators Salah, Masoud, Gamal and Flint, stay behind, the rest of you get to work.'

Well, that was music to my ears. I loved live events. You were far less restricted by time paradoxes or end of world scenarios. Time paradoxes were a huge problem. On one occasion a team screwed up so badly during a visit to England in 1647, that the quantum stepper wouldn't work for a year. By the time we stepped back, their timeline had twisted, and they'd had a whole thirty years where the English had had a civil war, assassinated their king—THEIR KING—and banned Christmas carols. Happily, the British are pretty resilient when it comes to their timeline, and it didn't take too long before they re-installed the monarchy and tried to pretend that it had all been a bit of an embarrassing interlude. That said, it was not one of our finer moments. Every cadet has to recite liturgical plainsong for an hour if they fail their Cause and Effect module. They don't get to fail it twice.

Sam started to take us through the case. The Q Field was giving hot lead locations for London, Cambridge and Poland.

We all groaned. Those northern countries were horrible in winter. Poland was likely to be covered in snow, London was going to be wet, and Cambridge was just going to be freezing with that cold wind blowing off the fens. Fingers crossed it ended up in Britain; much less chance of snow.

'What details do we have for the extraction event?'

'Right,' said Sam. 'It's a Fabergé egg, but not one we recognise. This makes it all the more important. Currently, we have it rolling out of someone's hand in Cambridge. As it hits the pavement it cracks and then rolls onto the road, where a passing bus runs over it.' We all winced.

'As it's live, I don't need to remind you that if you find the egg earlier, you can extract it immediately. This one has a quantum probability of zero per cent that it will survive.'

Basically, no matter what we did to try to fix the timeline, this egg was toast. This was typical of the rare and valuable stuff. Their own allure was often the cause of their inevitable downfall.

Even though we were all in a state of readiness, we needed to wait until a morning slot on the stepper. Now that we had the finer details, I sent everyone home to brush up on all the relevant information, as well as pack accordingly. We were going to set up base in London and move if need be. As northern cities go, I don't hate London, and it does have some lovely museums, it's just that the Thames always makes me feel sad; a river should have crocodiles.

As we headed out, I shouted a final warning not to drink. Drinking after a step was dumb. Who needed a quantum hangover with bizarre side effects? Drinking before one was dangerous.

I played with the idea of going off to Paul's. Whilst we were on a mission we would be strictly colleagues only. In the end, though I decided against it. I wanted to be on top form for tomorrow, and that meant a good night's sleep. And don't assume the obvious. We would just as often spend the whole night chatting. A few months ago, we'd sailed a felucca down the Nile for a few hundred miles. It was a pretty special time, and I began to see a whole new side to him. There's a book by Jane Austen, a Beta classic that we adore, with a character called Mr Darcy. He has a little sister that he utterly dotes on. Well, that was how Paul was about his sister. She is the world to him, and I was charmed by how devoted a brother he was. I've never wanted kids, but at that moment I suddenly saw what a great father he'd make. Heading home instead, I ran through all the latest briefings and finally got to bed at about two. So much for an early night.

The following morning both teams assembled in front of the Q Field. Paul and Ramin were a team, as were Clio and I, and I was going to be in overall control of both teams. I could see that Paul wasn't thrilled by that piece of news, but I had more experience and a better track record of successful retrievals. Sam had chosen me over Paul, and Paul had better not let Sam see his displeasure. Our boss had no time for people who questioned his judgement. I sympathised with Paul though. I hated it when I was passed over to lead an expedition. I just had to trust that Sam knew what he was doing.

We were travelling light. We had our bags of tricks, laser guns, wow bangs, first-aid kit... the essential stuff. The rest we would purchase and re-purpose when we got over there. We could easily adapt their technology, although I couldn't wait until they improved their capacity and speeds. They were still using microchips, so some days it was like playing with an abacus. Still, it was easier than travelling back to a pre-digital age, where we had to carry over more equipment and risk being discovered and called witches.

Most of our technology was stored in our wrist brace. It was our tether to home, and as long as that was on our wrist we could get back. Besides being our lifeboat, it was also a communicator and locator. Through the brace, we were linked. While on Beta we had no way to communicate with home, so it was essential we all keep in touch with each other. I smiled as I took in our suitcases. They had wheels on, which was a nice development for Beta. Not exactly hover technology, but better than having to lug poorly-designed, heavy cases from each arm. Everyone was dressed appropriately, which of course meant we were currently sweating profusely. Wardrobe had given Clio heels as requested. Added to her long leather swing coat, I thought she was a tad conspicuous, but Clio stood out anywhere. Her argument was that she may as well look good whilst doing it. We were stepping through the field into London so she wouldn't stand out too much, but I wouldn't send her to Poland. A tall Egyptian woman that had the poise of an ancient pharaoh would be pushing our luck. Although for a laugh I could order her to wear a cagoule and Doc Martens. Like I was. Ramin and Paul were both dressed in leisurewear; fancy tracksuits, hoodies and trainers that never saw the inside of a gym. Ramin was from Persia, Paul from France. Neither genotype should be an issue in London, but we'd probably need to keep Ramin out of the Home Counties.

Having run through a final briefing, Sam gave us the go-ahead and switched on the field. The plain white wall in front of us began to bulge and shimmer. Colours and sparks began to ripple across it, and as the safety bells started to chime, Clio and I walked towards the wall and stepped through.

#10 Charles – Beta Earth

Charlie rubbed his brogues on the back of his cords and caught his reflection in a high street window. Well dressed; expensive, but casual. A simple blazer over a tailored shirt, a leather belt and a pair of needlecord jeans. He wanted to portray money, not desperation. It was a known fact that people will give more money to people that look as though they don't need it. Charlie now needed to convince a total stranger that he was someone that could be trusted. He was cold-calling, but he wasn't coming empty handed. He had stopped at a Polish delicatessen and picked up some cakes. Charlie was hoping that a bit of childhood nostalgia might sweeten the old boy.

Leaving the high street behind, he headed down a residential street of smart Victorian terraces. Each property was well maintained, with a range of garden styles out the front. All were uniformly small, but in this area of London, they were worth their weight in gold. Charlie knocked with the brass knocker. Through the stained glass, he could see a figure approach the door. An old man opened the inner porch door and peered out through the glass of the front door.

'What do you want?'

Hmm, a naturally suspicious and distrustful character. What approach to take? Charlie recalibrated his "journalist looking for a bird" story and decided to go with the truth. Well, most of it.

'Philip Guscott? I've come from your sister-in-law. Pani Zofia Guskov.'

There was a pause, and then Philip stepped forward and opened the door. He seemed suspicious and to be debating whether to send him away. 'And I've brought some Napoleonka?' He held the bag up, smiling. 'Have I pronounced that correctly?'

Philip's eyes immediately lit up. Who could resist cake? 'Pah, these modern bakers have no idea. Still, they may be tolerable. Come in.'

Introducing himself, Charlie was shown through to a well-lit front room. Heading out to the kitchen, Philip put the kettle on and pulled out some forks and side plates for the two slices of cake. Charlie offered to help but was waved into the front room, and whilst he waited he had a look around. It was an elegant room with an almost prissy level of perfection. This was the space of an avowed bachelor. The shelves were full of history and wildlife titles. A few of the history titles rang gentle warning bells, and he began to wonder about the rift between the two brothers. A collection of Leni Riefenstahl was curious; the thumbed copy of Mein Kampf seemed a little more problematic.

Zofia had told Charlie that her husband had stayed in Poland to help rebuild the country. Had Filip left because he was ashamed of his fellow Poles, or because he feared them turning on him? Not all who'd fled were innocents.

'So how is Zofia? I can't think when I last thought of her. Does she still live in that little flat in Warsaw?'

Charlie smiled sadly. 'That was indeed where I met her, but I'm afraid to say that I heard the other day that she had died. I was coming to see you on another matter but thought you might prefer to hear the news from someone that had recently spoken to her. Rather than a social worker or police officer, I mean. Or worse yet, a letter through the post.'

'So, she is dead then.' He took a bite of the cake and smiled. 'This is very good, you know. Try some.' Taking another bite, he smiled as Charlie followed suit and made an appreciative noise.

'Are you shocked that I am not sadder? You young people think death is such an awful thing, but at my age, it is our constant companion. Besides which I never much cared for her when I knew her. She was always wittering about politics. Life was hard enough without outsiders taking our jobs from us and people like her taking their side.'

Charlie nodded in agreement and continued to make small talk, commenting on the fact that Philip's English was so good he couldn't even hear an accent.

'Time smooths out most things. Plus, some people cling onto their accents, as though it is all they have left of the old country. If they loved the motherland so much, why leave?' Philip lifted his palms and shrugged. The perfect immigrant.

Charlie thought about that; did time smooth things out or did it just help you forget about them? The more the two men chatted, the more convinced Charlie was that he was in the presence of a Nazi sympathiser and that this was the nature of the brothers' fall out. Charlie blessed his tall blonde physique. It had no doubt helped him through the front door. Did their grandfather know about Filip's political persuasions? Did he care?

'But enough of these things,' said Philip, wiping crumbs from his lips. 'What can I do for you?'

'Right, the thing is, I collect Russian folk art and I was in Warsaw where I met your sister-in-law. She told me that she had a matryoshka set she wanted to sell.'

Charlie paused as Philip nodded his head. 'Did she still have that doll set then? It was my brother's you know.'

'So, she said. Well, I told her I didn't want it as it wasn't complete, but you know what her flat is like. If I'm honest, I felt a bit sorry for her.'

'She married the wrong brother and no mistake. Not that she was ever my type. No vision. Still, as you say, it's very sad.' Charlie offered him another slice of cake, which he happily accepted, and poured them both another cup of tea.

'The thing is, as I was leaving, she said that the last she knew was that you had the outer doll. That your grandfather had split them between the two of you?'

'And you want to know if I still have it? Forty years later. And now you've tracked me down? Boy, you must want it really badly.'

Charlie put his cup back on its saucer. 'What can I say? You see through me. It's worth more if it's complete.'

Philip roared with laughter, or at least his tired, wheezy lungs tried. Coughing, he struggled for breath and dabbed his eyes on his shirt cuff. 'You have to get out of bed early to catch me out.'

Charlie nodded. This was all part of the game. Let the punter think they had the upper hand. 'Fair enough. It's not like you still have it after all this time, but I'm happy to pay for any information you can give me as to where it went?'

'If I could tell you where it is right now, what would it be worth?'

Charlie relaxed. This push and pull was all part of the game. Either he knew something, or he didn't. Charlie could wait. Asking what the information was worth was a clear sign that if he had the doll, he was prepared to sell it.

'Depends on how decent the lead is. If you tell me you sold it in Covent Garden in the sixties, I'd give you twenty pounds. If you tell me you threw it in the bin, I'd give you fifty. If you told me you gave it to Oxfam last month, I'd offer you a hundred.'

'Why fifty if it's in the bin?'

'Because then I'll stop wasting my time. And that's worth something to me, and I'd be grateful to you.'

'And if I can tell you its exact location?'

Charlie tried to sit still. 'I don't know, a hundred and fifty?' He sipped his tea and tried not to wince as he burnt his tongue.

Philip chuckled to himself. 'I think you've overplayed your hand, young man. Have a look in the back of the dresser behind you. On the left-hand side.'

Charlie got out of his chair and dug around in the dresser. Moving stacks of tableware, canteens and decanters aside, he could make something out at the back. There, right in the back corner, was a large wooden doll. The light was poor, but it looked like the same artwork as the matryoshka set he had back in Cambridge. He went to pick it up and his hands nearly shook as he realised it was heavy. Far heavier than an empty wooden case should be. Moving items aside, he gently pulled it forward and then placed it on the coffee table between the two men.

'There it is then.'

'You owe me a hundred and fifty pounds.'

Charlie laughed and opened his wallet, handing over a few notes and making sure Philip saw the rest of the stack.

'It is heavy, yes? You noticed that?'

Charlie just nodded. He didn't want to discuss the weight of the doll.

'That is down to my grandfather. He filled it with soil and glued it shut.' He said I wasn't to open it until my brother and I were reunited and he had the rest of the dolls with him. He said we would be rewarded. This is the soil of our motherland so we could plant a new seed and heal the family tree. That family was the most valuable gift there was.'

Philip shrugged and shook his head. 'What can I say? My grandfather was Russian. Proud and brave, but like all Russians, he tended towards the dramatic or the romantic. I chose to honour my grandfather, but I would not make the first move. As for my brother, he was a coward and a traitor. We had a new future in the grasp of our hands, and all we needed to do was make a fist and grab it. Clean the country out and allow it to rise once more.'

Philip was beginning to get agitated, and Charlie needed to keep things on a friendly keel. Plus, he didn't want his revulsion to show.

'Ah well. I'll leave you to it then and thank you for a very fine cup of tea. I've always thought that the Russians could teach the English a thing or two about tea making. It's clearly in the blood.'

He began to tidy up his plate and saucer as Philip looked alarmed.

'Don't you want it then?'

Charlie acted surprised. 'I thought if you had kept it all this time, that maybe it did mean something to you after all?'

Charlie kept his face blank as Philip rapidly began to backtrack. 'Well, you came all this way, and besides, it has been gathering dust all these years. I am prepared to sell it if the price is right?'

'Look, Mr Guscott, I have to be honest, it would be great to have it but now you tell me it's damaged. I'm going to have to take it to a specialist to unseal it. That's going to cost me. I've already paid you one fifty. It's all digging into a dwindling profit margin.' He sighed and waited. This was tricky. He'd pay any price to have the doll. He didn't even know if there was an egg hidden in there, but now he was too caught up in the thrill of the chase. However, if Philip got a whiff of that, then he might not sell it at all.

'A hundred pounds and it's yours.'

Charlie paused. A complete matryoshka set fully restored could possibly sell for a thousand if he took it to the right dealer. Russian folk art was beginning to be gobbled up by the oligarchs. And of course, it might be something else altogether.

'Okay, let's shake on it.'

The drive home had nearly killed Charlie, and he closed his front door with an air of relief, the tension leaving his shoulders. His front door opened into a nicely furnished living room with a big squishy sofa and a large TV for his Xbox, but he headed into the study. It faced north and the window overlooked his courtyard. Even so, he drew the curtain before taking the doll out of his haversack.

Pulling open a drawer, he retrieved some fine tools and set to work on the seal. He was used to working on artefacts and had acquired a set of small tools and the skills required for small restorations and repairs. Swollen joints, rust, dirt, even barnacles; all could be fixed with patience and a little bit of knowledge.

An hour later he felt the last bit of glue give way. He put his tools away and wiped his palms on the leg of his trousers. Very slowly he cupped the top of the doll and gently twisted it; sand, not soil, began to pour out over the table. Clearly, the story about soil from the motherland was just a ruse. Charlie continued to carefully lift the doll. Then, as the top of the doll was removed, Charlie watched as the sand poured away from the edges of a jewel-encrusted egg.

For a few seconds, he just sat and stared at it in wonder.

Very gently, Charlie lifted the egg out and was surprised by the weight of it. It was a white enamelled egg, with the towers of St Basil inlaid in colourful enamel. At the top of the egg sat a gold orthodox cross. Around the lower circumference of the egg was a band of pearls and diamonds. This band acted as the base of the cathedral. Below the band was a filigree network of platinum threads and more diamonds and pearls. Charlie looked at it in wonder. It was exquisite, and though he had never heard of any description that matched this, he felt certain he was looking at a piece of work by Fabergé. He looked carefully at the cross. Did it pull up to reveal the surprise? Was there a hidden button?

He picked up the egg, intrigued by how solid it felt. Those pearls and diamonds looked so fragile, and yet in reality they were not going anywhere. Even so, Charlie held the egg with a level of reverence. Not only was the artistry incredible, it was likely worth over twenty million pounds. Still, could he work out how to open the egg? He smiled to himself. Could it be so simple? Holding the top and bottom of the egg, he gently twisted it and grinned as the two halves came apart. Just like the Russian doll.

Removing the top half of the egg, he revealed a second egg, this time featuring two portraits of the tsar and tsarina, each portrait looking towards each other. Both were smiling. This was easily the most intimate image he had ever seen of the tsarina. Her hair was down, and she was gazing at the man she loved. Again, this egg was inlaid with enamel and jewels and another central band. Charlie twisted again and revealed the next egg. A portrait of their eldest daughter, the Grand Duchess Olga, reading a book. This egg was made of etched gold, and the filigree was studded with sapphires. As each egg revealed another daughter, Charlie studied the family line. Fabergé had designed the eggs to have a flat bottom so that they could all stand upright. At last, he held the Anastasia egg in his hand, the Romanov's fourth and final daughter. By now the egg was only an inch tall, and yet its size did not diminish the skill of the miniature portrait. Twisting gently, Charlie saw that the final object was not an egg but a large, polished blood-red ruby that had the image of Tsarevich Alexei carved into it, the tragic little prince who carried all the hopes of the Romanov bloodline, whilst also carrying the painful and life-threatening haemophilia within that same precious blood.

This wasn't just a Fabergé egg. This was six Fabergé eggs, and at the heart rested a child of blood. It wasn't just a rare jewel but an intimate family portrait, all bound and protected under the eyes of God as represented by St Basil's basilica. Looking from the outside, no one would guess at the personal story within.

This was incredibly intimate, and Charlie felt certain that the tsarina had kept this egg with her at all times. Even at her death. Looking at it now, Charlie realised that this was going to fetch far more than twenty million, though he would settle for far less, so long as it went to a public museum. This was the find of the century, and he was excited to break the bloody curse of the Romanovs.

Interlude 1

The following text conversation was retrieved, doing a sweep of the ghost files of the Q Zone security system. It has been added to the evidence report for Case No: 234530/H. As yet neither correspondent has been identified.

- We want the egg.
- It will be tricky. Live Events are closely monitored and attract additional personnel.
- Is this of any interest to us?
- Just saying we may not be able to acquire it for you.
- Unacceptable.
- It's just…
- We want the egg, not excuses.

#11 Neith – Beta Earth

As soon as we'd stepped through, I slapped my wrist brace and the perception filter buzzed into effect, the vibration fields knocking out any surveillance cameras. You never quite knew where you were going to come out, and it was essential to be able to take stock without frightened locals running away. Sadly, there was nothing I could do about the rain soaking my hair, other than pulling my cagoule hood up over my head. I checked my location and time—Goodge Street, Wednesday 10th January—two weeks before the egg was due to be destroyed. Perfect. I offered a quick thanks to the Q Field and then checked on the location of the others. I could see Clio across the street and waved at her. Paul was a street away. Happily, the Q Field never dropped us in the path of moving objects. Ramin had arrived a few hours ahead of us, which was a minor glitch but had worked in our favour. He had already booked us into a hotel and nipped out to Charing Cross Road to buy laptops and modems. We'd go out and get more soon, but in the meantime, we had enough to start running our own software and our larger security system.

Once the four of us had settled in, Paul and Ramin had booked the next available flight over to Warsaw. It was a slim chance, but we might be able to get a lead on the location of the egg. The Q Field told us a Zofia

Guskov and an Englishman were connected to the treasure. In its usual oblique way, it hadn't supplied any further information. I'd checked the internet when we'd arrived, but the discovery of a missing Fabergé egg hadn't hit the headlines, so we had to assume the Q Field was leaving out some pertinent information. As usual. Clio, Paul and I joined Ramin at the hotel and began to work. That had been the previous day, and now I was waiting to hear from Ramin and Paul whilst Clio and I monitored the local media.

Clio walked through from the hotel bedroom into our living room. We had set up in a large hotel apartment in the Mondrian. They are great at not asking questions.

There was a knock on the door and I groaned.

'Clio, I'm not kidding, if you've ordered from room service one more time, I'm going to have to write you up!' There wasn't an issue with room service as such, but I didn't like the constant stream of hotel staff coming in. Hotels like this were discreet, but I didn't want to push our luck.

She rolled her eyes at me as the waiter brought in a tray covered in salmon sandwiches and petits fours.

'You don't have to eat them.'

I sighed and flipped open the laptop again. I was fidgety, waiting for news from the boys. If we were lucky, they'd be successful, and we could all step back from our respective locations. If we weren't, then they would need to fly back over here and we'd continue the hunt together. Once we had stepped over to Beta Earth we were on our own. There was no leaning through the portal to grab something useful or using it like a bridge to travel quickly across the globe. That's why successful missions relied on perfect planning and great quartermasters. I was proud to be working with one of the best, when she wasn't licking icing off her fingers.

'Cat's teeth, Clio! How many have you eaten already?'

She shrugged. She wasn't wrong, there wasn't much else to do. We were fully set up; we had caught up with the local political social structure and were now waiting for news from Poland. As usual, Beta Earth was full of depressing news stories of death and despair, but there were also acts of great beauty and discovery.

Clearly, Alpha Earth is the better version, but we seem to miss that spark that creates the extraordinary, or maybe it just stands out more here because of all the awfulness. One thing we had less of in Alpha was the sublime. If we drew something, it was pretty, and people appreciated it. On Beta, the painting was imbued with passion, with blood and fear, with rapture and awe. We just didn't do those extremes. And in our culture, that showed. Maybe that's why we appreciated Beta's stuff more than they did.

My earpiece buzzed and I tapped Ramin's call through. I called out to Clio, who was now cleaning the guns and preparing our first-aid kits. We didn't plan on getting shot, but our guns fired electrical pulses which caused a heart to spasm. It generally never killed anyone, but it stopped them in much the same way that a house falling on your head would. Our version left no trace though. Beta guns on the other hand ripped through skin and bones, leaving blood leaking all over the place and an unacceptably high possibility of death. Our technology still hadn't mastered portable forcefields, so we had to rely on speed, general superiority, great triage kits and not getting shot at in the first place.

As soon as Clio joined me I flicked on the projection. Ramin was standing in front of us. Behind him, we could just about make out the River Vistula. Again, he had chosen a hotel on the river. We just couldn't help it. Besides, a river made for a quick getaway in a crisis. Confirming that the room was contained, I told him to report.

'It's not here. Paul went to the location of the hotspot, but the lead was dead.'

'Dead?'

'Literally.' Paul stepped into view. 'When I got to the suggested address, the police were there. I stepped away until they had gone and then came back to chat to the neighbours. Turns out it was the residence of an old woman called Zofia Guskov, the lead we had. Neighbours said that prior to her death, she had met an Englishman called Charles Bradshaw. Zofia had given her neighbour his calling card, saying he paid well for old tat. They couldn't tell me anything more, but I think the combination of mysterious death and English stranger suggests I was at the right location.'

'Did the neighbour pass on this man's name to the police?' asked Clio.

Paul laughed. 'No. The neighbour has very clear views on the police.'

I praised the guys on their intel gathering, especially getting the name of the Englishman. That was a real lead.

'Right, get back over here as fast as you can. Clio and I will spend the rest of the day tracking down this Charles and then we'll make plans when you're back.'

Switching off, I looked over to Clio who was already typing away on her keyboard, writing subroutines to hack into various websites including Google and Facebook. Between the two of them, we could cover most people in the UK.

I decided to go for a run. When I got to the foyer, I was gutted to discover great big flakes of snow falling. I ran along the embankment for a while and then gave up. The pavement was becoming slippery and everyone was waving umbrellas around like they were lethal weapons. I grabbed a hot chocolate, one of the things I did love about being here, and sloped back to the hotel. A news kiosk proclaimed that a dolphin had been seen in the Thames yesterday. It wasn't a crocodile, but it was good news. For a few decades, it had looked as though they had managed to destroy their river. We couldn't rescue geological features, and we had all watched in misery as they frittered it away. Now life was returning, and it couldn't help but cheer us up, even if it was so cold that my gooseflesh now had gooseflesh. The hotel had a steam room, so, finishing my drink I headed off to warm up in there instead and try to unknit my freezing joints.

Once I felt vaguely human again I headed back to the room. Clio had been researching Cambridge as the extraction point for the egg. Every scenario showed it ending there. But if we could snatch it quietly before the big finale, so much the better. Fewer ripples in the young timeline.

The room was beautifully warm and there were various plates of canapés dotted around. Clio had got busy with room service again. The joy of an expensive hotel was that they never so much as blinked an eye when you put in strange requests. Like her request for French Fancies. That girl did love those little sponge cakes.

'Did you know you can get just these by the box load?' she said waving the little cake at me. 'I ordered some dim sum as well. They're on that tray by your laptop and the cafetière has Ethiopian roast in it.'

The joy of having your best friend as your partner.

'Did your jog take you further than the sauna?'

I ignored the sarcasm and referred her to the snow. 'It doesn't help things, does it?'

It could clear up later or gridlock the whole city. Beta Britain was full-on rubbish with snow. They could see how other countries dealt with it, but they failed to implement the same measures. Their reasoning was that those measures were simply not cost effective for just a couple of days every other year. It was almost as if they enjoyed the chaos and closures.

As I powered up my laptop, Clio shared her intel on Cambridge and then we decided to find an earlier extraction point. The other problem with a live shot is that if we missed the egg's extraction point, that was it. We failed.

'Okay. Let's start at the beginning,' I said. 'We know Charles Bradshaw met with Zofia Guskov. According to the Q Field, the egg moves from Poland to Cambridge. I think it's safe to assume that Zofia passed the egg to Charles?'

'Not necessarily,' said Clio. 'Maybe she passed him information? Maybe she was unaware of the egg altogether. After all, if she knew she was sitting on a fortune would she give it away to a stranger?'

Clio's logic was sound. 'Okay then, Charles may not yet have the egg. Or he may. Either way, what do we think he'll do if he gets it? We need to look into him. Is he the sort to keep it, sell it or donate it? Clio, start seeing if you can spot any hints about a Fabergé coming onto the market. I think for something like this people will be very cagey, but if anyone can get behind the firewalls and break down odd patterns, it's you. I'm going to investigate Charles. I have his number on his card and that should be more than enough for me to find out all there is to know about him.'

I pulled my laptop towards me. Finding stuff on Charles was the easy part. Clio had to search the internet for oddities. Things that struck a wrong note. On the internet, you can imagine the problem. Plus, all those kitten videos were like catnip to two Egyptian girls. But Clio was one of our best researchers and wasn't going to be daunted by too much information. Better than too little. You should have seen her trying to make her way around Roanoke. I hated that job. We all did. The less said about it, the better. It was distressing, and all we had been able to save were a few books. Don't get me wrong. Books are incredibly important but watching an entire colony die was hard.

I stopped musing and started searching. After a few hours, I had Charles Bradshaw's entire life on my laptop. By habit, he searched with his privacy filter on, which was no hindrance to us. But he made few phone calls and never backed up his phone. He also had a very low image trace; he must keep all his photos on his phone and he never posted on social media.

'What about calls?' asked Clio.

'Not from this phone. He either has a burner phone, or he uses the postal system.' Neither of which I could intercept. Well, I could intercept a burner phone, but I'd need the number. 'How're you doing?'

Clio threw a French Fancy at me in frustration and continued to type. I left her to it as she scribbled notes and swore quietly. I had dug up a few leads from Charles' end that might help narrow her haystack, but it was still a big field. Charles was from Cambridge, which helped secure him in our mind as the principal target. He worked for a museum, which strengthened the donation idea, but he had a track record of buying and selling beyond the remit of his employers' purview. That solidified the idea that he was going to try to sell it privately.

Getting up, I poured her a fresh coffee and having stretched my legs again, I returned to the laptop to see if I could find evidence of a burner phone.

'Got it!' Clio broke the silence that had settled over the room as we pored over our screens. 'One of the auction houses you gave me. I was tracking all their employees and I noticed a Carl Ponsonby had been complaining on Facebook about a toothache all week. Agony apparently, although his girlfriend seemed less concerned. Anyway, he booked the day off work for a dental appointment tomorrow. I cross-checked it and yesterday the dental practice received a call from him cancelling the appointment. He hasn't been on social media since.'

That sounded promising. 'What's his specialism?'

'Rare gems, Chinese jade, and, drum roll, ladies and gentlemen, the House of Fabergé.' Clio sat back grinning. We had our connection. 'Let's see Ramin's face when I tell him we have Charles' contact already.'

It was a toss-up between the two of them as to which was the better researcher. Of course, they weren't in competition with each other, but there was no point in telling them that. I had never met Ramin's equal until I met Clio. She was like a computer, being able to take random, unconnected data and extrapolate the most likely scenario or interpretation. If she thought Carl Ponsonby was our lead, then that was good enough for me.

The door opened and I jumped up. Paul had contacted us earlier; the flight had landed without a hitch, obviously, but with snow, you could never tell at which point this country would choose to collapse. Opening the door, both men piled in with their luggage and a barrage of complaints.

'You know, there's two foot of snow in Poland and no one blinks an eye, country running like clockwork. It hasn't even settled here, and the taxi driver wanted to charge double in case he got stuck!' Paul seemed particularly manic, but I know he didn't like the cold either so maybe this assignment was getting to him. As they headed into their rooms, Ramin called out over his shoulder.

'By the way, look into a Carl Ponsonby. I reckon he could be our next lead.'

I ducked as a French Fancy hit their bedroom door.

#12 Neith – Beta Earth

We still didn't know where or when the meeting between Carl Ponsonby and Charles Bradshaw was going to take place, so we split into teams to shadow each man. I gave the auction employee to the boys. As he lived in London, they could have a pause from travelling. Clio and I would tail Bradshaw. At four am, we boosted a car from a long stay car park, headed up the M11 to Cambridge and parked outside his street. We were wearing heated suits, but let me tell you, sitting in a car at five am in Cambridge is still bloody cold.

Eventually, just after eight a man fitting Charles Bradshaw's description left the registered address for one Charles Bradshaw. It was good enough for us. He had on a big padded jacket and a satchel slung in front of his body that he kept cradled close to him. Telling Clio to follow in the car, I got out and followed on foot. He was looking around a lot, but he didn't notice me. Why would he? I just looked like a short female student making my way to early morning lectures with my arms wrapped around my satchel and a scarf across my face. No need for fancy theatrics today.

I followed him into the train station; he might not think anyone was following him, but he sure was acting suspiciously. He sat down without buying a ticket.

'Clio, ditch the car. I think he's getting ready to catch a train as it pulls out. Best guess, London train, platform one. Get on it.'

A few minutes later, I watched as Clio walked into the train station. She looked up at the screens and then got onto the train that was idling at the far platform. An announcement over the tannoy declared that the eight thirty from Cambridge was preparing to depart.

My earpiece hissed and I heard Clio's voice. 'Is he getting on this train? We've just had a carriage announcement saying we were preparing to leave. I'm not going to be much use stuck on the wrong train.'

I looked over and Charles was still reading a paper. Had we got it wrong? Was he meeting someone else, somewhere else? Just as I was doubting myself, he sprang up and headed briskly towards platform one.

'He's heading your way. Following!'

I stopped talking and now ran past him, shouting out to the conductor, every inch the last-minute student, and leapt onto the train. A few seconds later he also got on and walked past me down the middle of the carriage in search of a seat. Given how rammed the train was, I thought he was on a hiding to nothing. I messaged the boys that the three of us were indeed heading to London, then began to relax.

Watching the countryside roll by, I sent out hugs of sympathy to the cattle that were standing in the white frosted fields. Calling Clio, I asked what she had done with the car and was pleased to hear it was currently being valeted and refuelled. She had also left them the number of the private garage she had "borrowed" it from. I wondered if the owner would ever know about its short disappearance.

Arriving in London, Clio and I re-grouped and watched as Charles pulled a phone out and tapped in a short text, then headed towards the taxi rank, commuters and tourists swirling around him.

Ramin's voice now buzzed in my ear. 'Ponsonby's just received a text message from an unknown number and he then googled directions to a café near St Paul's.'

We ran down to the tubes. Now that we had a destination, we could afford to lose visual contact. With morning traffic, we could be sitting in the café by the time either man arrived if we took the train.

'Ramin. Can you safely turn all the traffic lights to red for a bit? Let's slow down London for a few minutes.'

Just under an hour later, I speared a piece of black pudding. This was one of the highlights of a British assignment, the breakfast. I knew it was unhealthy and unethical and according to many, morally bankrupt, but I stole things and shot people for a living. It was practically a given that I was going to eat meat.

Charles walked into the café and sat down at a window table. As he arrived, the owner waved at him and came over to remove the reserved sign. Clio scowled, and I had to reassure her that not everything was available online. If she'd had a few weeks to tail

Charles in the flesh, she'd have known about this friendship. As it was, we were here anyway. No harm, no foul.

A man walked in and Charles nodded at him. Carl Ponsonby pulled out a chair and sat down as the waitress came over to take his order. Ramin followed shortly after and went to the counter, ordering a pot of tea, and choosing a table on the other side of the room. Paul was outside somewhere, covering the street. Clio dabbed her lips with her napkin and headed to the back, ostensibly to use the loos, but in reality covering the rear exit.

The team was now in place. If Charles were carrying the egg, we would lift it here and head home.

'Any sign of the egg?'

What the hell was wrong with Paul? He knew better than to communicate during a potential extraction. I needed vigilance from the team, not chatter. When there was a sign, I would let them know. I ignored the comment and nearly flinched when he repeated his query.

Leaning over my Sudoku and allowing my hair to cover my mouth, I told him to shut the fuck up and continued to mark up my newspaper whilst carefully watching their table.

'Okay,' I muttered, 'Bradshaw, has just placed a large Russian doll on the table… Right, now he's returned it to his satchel… Charles is showing Ponsonby something in his fist.'

Heads turned in the café as a man swore out loud and then, laughing, he apologised to the rest of the patrons.

'Right. Looks like our boy does have the egg. All units ready. When they leave the café we will lift him, sedate him, remove the doll and—'

Whatever else I was going to say never made it past the screech of tyres. Out on the road, a car had pulled to a stop and the glass-fronted café exploded in a hail of gunfire. Charles' and Carl's bodies flew back as shards of glass and bullets tore into them. Ramin grabbed one of the customers, shielding her as I ran towards the satchel. One of the men from the car was already ahead of me. He stepped through the broken frame and tried to kick me in the face as I lunged forward. Sliding under his foot, I twisted and shot him, but my gun appeared to have no effect. He threw the bag through the window to someone standing in the street. Grabbing a knife strapped to my thigh I stabbed at him, but only succeeded in propelling him forward. Beneath his clothing he must have been wearing Kevlar. Both men scrambled back into the car and screamed away again, rubber smoking on the road. It had all happened so fast that the glass was still falling out of the window frame.

'Paul, Clio, hotel now! Monitor all emergency band waves and traffic reports. Find that car. We'll join you in a minute. Ramin's tending to some of the injured. Ponsonby and Bradshaw are dead.'

Having given my instructions, I now slid into the role of terrified bystander and ran screaming with the other patrons to the loos at the back of the café. In the panic, no one noticed as I slid away through the kitchen. Jogging around to the front, I joined the rubberneckers that had already started to form a crowd. Ramin came out through the shattered front door and laid a woman down, calling for help as he did so. As people rushed forward, he got up and walked away. I followed, and as we turned the corner, we linked arms and started laughing. Just another couple wandering through London as the sirens approached.

#13 Julius – Beta Earth

Julius pushed the books back and decided to head to the refectory early. It was no good, he just couldn't concentrate. He hadn't heard from Charlie in days. He didn't think Charlie was going to find an egg, but it was still quite exciting to think about it. If he had found it though, it would explain the radio silence. A find this important would not be talked about for fear of the wrong parties getting wind of it: Russian oligarchs, billionaire sheikhs, Chinese triads.

Julius grinned. This was more James Bond than Indiana Jones, but this was Julius' life, lived vicariously through his friend. And this was typical Charlie, blowing in all full of excitement and then disappearing for months on end. He would hint to Julius that he was on the trail of something massive, and the next thing Julius would hear about it, it was part of a museum tour. Sometimes over a bottle of red wine, Charlie would share a hair-raising tale of recovery, though usually, it was only the beginning and the end. No middle.

Occasionally some of Charlie's deals were said to be a bit close to the bone. Maybe a secondary artefact was also found, but that didn't make it to the open market or the museums. Julius took those stories with a pinch of salt; Charlie had an excellent reputation and there were always people ready to put the knife in. Charlie played fast and loose, but he was essentially honest. If the museums turned down a piece he'd offered them, then why shouldn't he sell it? God knows the wages paid to curators and researchers was hardly impressive. He was regularly offered private employment for eye-watering sums of money, but Charlie knew those artefacts never made it to the light of day. He also knew that his potential employers didn't care how an item was acquired. Playing fast and loose with the law was fine. Breaking it wasn't.

The college refectory was loud and busy, with lots of students milling around, grabbing something to eat before the next lecture. Julius waved at some colleagues and went to join them. Some company and chat would help him refocus. He needed to submit his paper next week and now he was behind, thanks to Charlie's egg hunt. Dan was an expert in the renaissance period, as was Wendy, and even if they didn't talk shop it would be an engaging lunch. Whilst Julius' field was religious systems, linguistics and folklore, he still found most subjects to be fascinating. Especially when the people talking about them were knowledgeable and enthusiastic. Besides which, Wendy was also on the rowing team and regularly had fun tales about near collisions and battles with swans. Smiling, she shuffled along the bench. Julius stepped over and sat down beside her, catching up on what Dan, opposite, was talking about with great animation.

'…well, you know, you can't tell a fresher!'

Julius nodded agreement and tucked into his sandwiches. He was on a pure research year and wouldn't have any teaching element until next year. Freshers didn't tend to bother him. First-year students either got on with it, or they didn't. He didn't feel the frustrations that some of his colleagues did, but he suspected that was because he didn't care as much. He was only interested when they were. Too often in the first year, they were adapting to the fact that everyone else was either brilliant or a phenomenally hard worker, sometimes both. They had lost the thing that had made them stand out in school and were loudly and desperately trying to find another one. The ones that generally succeeded through the maelstrom of Cambridge were the ones that hadn't been bothered by their achievements in the first place. They were here because they loved learning and were deeply curious about their subject. It was easy to feel intimidated and overwhelmed by the loud confidence of many of the students, but gradually people found their feet and settled in. Or left.

One such leaver, Miles, now hurried towards them across the hall. He had misjudged the balance between working hard and playing hard and had dropped out at the end of the second year. He had been reading English, as well as working on the student newsletter and as a stringer for some London tabloids. Eventually, his studies suffered as he partied harder and submitted more tabloid copy than academic essays. Push came to shove, and he dropped out and started earning. Now he was a full-time journalist and published author. And a total gossip.

'Guys, guess what. You know Charles Bradshaw? The black market smuggler?'

Julius interrupted him. That was too much. 'We're friends and colleagues, Miles, not pundits. Charles is a curator and buyer that works in the field, recovering and retrieving lost or damaged artefacts. He is not a 'black market smuggler' for God's sake.'

Miles shot him a quick scowl but recovered. 'Oh, hi Julius, yes I forgot, you two went to school together, didn't you?' He managed to say it in a way that implied that old school ties would naturally blind a person to a friend's failings, or that the old school ties would be so strong that any wrongdoing would be simply ignored. It was a stock in trade catch-all for the gutter press when they wanted to dismiss a person's supporters.

'Well, I think this might change your mind. He's dead!'

Miles was gratified by the reaction of his audience and continued.

'Gunned down in a hail of bullets!'

'What?' Julius shivered.

'Drive-by shooting in London. He and another man were the clear targets. Police are baffled.'

'My God!' said Dan, looking at Julius with concern.

'I know. Police want to talk to a suspicious man who was seen talking to the driver of the car just minutes earlier. A man of Arabic appearance was also seen administering first aid in the café itself. He's disappeared! Police have not yet ruled out terrorism.'

Julius felt sick. Miles was talking in sensationalist headlines about one of his oldest friends. 'Excuse me.'

'Oh dear, bit too real world for you? Locked away in your ivory tower?'

'For Christ's sake, Miles,' said Wendy, 'Julius and Charles didn't just go to the same school, they were friends. He was in town just the other day.'

Miles was instantly alert. 'Got a quote? How are you feeling? When you spoke to him the other day, did you have an impending sense of doom?'

Julius stood up. He needed to get away from Miles' poisonous glee; the words were running into black oily sludge and he needed some fresh air.

'Mate. You can be off the record? What about an exclusive...'

Julius was already heading out of the dining hall and sat down on one of the benches beneath a stand of trees. He caught his breath and sat with his head in his hands, trying not to be sick. Charlie might have been loud and frustrating and often annoying, but he was also fun and kind and interesting, and he didn't deserve to be killed. Despite Julius' scepticism, it would appear that Charlie must have been on the track of the Fabergé egg. In fact, it seemed that he was not just on the trail, but that he might have actually found the egg. Why would he have been shot if he didn't have it?

Instead of wildly speculating, he returned to his study and opened the BBC news pages. Hopefully, there would be no salacious comments or vivid photos. Julius didn't think he could cope with actual graphics of his friend's final moments. Reading the news, he was appalled by the brutality of the attack.

A drive-by shooting had occurred in the morning at a small London café. Two male victims were at the same table and, as yet, not formally identified. Other people injured in the attack were stable and recovering in hospital. The car involved in the shooting had been found dumped nearby and the assailants had disappeared. As yet, the reason for the shooting was unclear. Eyewitness reports suggested that one of the men in the car grabbed a bag from one of the two men at the table. The BBC article stressed that this had not been confirmed by the police.

Julius sat back. This still seemed unreal, and he needed to try to understand what had happened. Closing down his computer, he decided to head home and pick up his spare keys for Charlie's house. Maybe he could find some clues there.

Leaning his bike against his front window, he found a note had been pushed through his letterbox asking him to contact the police to assist them in an on-going enquiry. He was surprised at the speed of contact, but it was a dramatic event. Whatever Hollywood would have its audience believe, drive-by shootings were extremely rare occurrences, even in London. No doubt the police were already heading to his workplace to see if they could find him there. He considered going back to work or calling them, but he decided to check out Charlie's house first. After all, if he discovered anything, he'd be able to give the police more information to help them track down Charlie's murderers. He knew the police wouldn't tell him anything, and that wasn't good enough. Julius wanted answers.

#14 Neith – Beta Earth

'What the fuck! I mean what the actual fuck?'

We were all sat around the table in our hotel room. I hate it when a mission includes dead people. It happens, I know it happens, but it always, without fail, feels like a catastrophic failure. Here we are in the business of collecting unique treasures, and we lose two people right in front of us. Obviously, saving the inhabitants on Beta Earth is not our remit, and besides, that would be a task of Sisyphean proportions. But still, to see them dying up close and personal, pumping out blood is never great.

'I still don't understand how it got out of our control so quickly,' said Clio. Acting as backstop, she'd had no eyes on the situation, but she had her head-piece in, as we all did.

'The thing is, Clio, we had no warning and the thing about that is, and I'm desperately trying not to look at Paul right now, but seriously, Paul? Did the big, fast, noisy car just tiptoe past you?'

'Of course I saw it. It just didn't seem suspicious.' Paul got up and was pacing around the room.

'And on reflection? How suspicious did it seem a minute later?' He glared at me. It was moments like this that he always resented, when I challenged him. I was in charge here and it was going to be me that would be responsible for any cock-up when I got home. The minute we stepped back, questions would be asked, and the buck stopped with me. So damn right I was going to challenge my team. If they screwed up, it was me that was going to carry the can.

'There's an eyewitness saying he saw the people in the car stop and talk to a man prior to it accelerating towards the café. Who was that? Can you at least describe him?'

'There wasn't anyone.'

'In the name of Ra, Paul! You didn't see the car. You didn't see the man. Just exactly what were you doing?'

'Neith—'

'And you can knock that off as well,' I said, cutting across Ramin. 'You stopped to administer first aid in a crowded room of witnesses. You had zero level of masking on! I can't use you in public now, and you have blown any future steps into this timeline.'

'Her mother was about to pull that shard of glass out of her thigh. I wasn't about to witness a third death just because some woman doesn't understand the function of the femoral artery. If I've blown this timeline for me and my partner, then I take full responsibly for that. But if we replayed this morning, I'd do it again. And a thousand times again. And so would you.'

We fell into an angry silence. Paul was still pacing and looking livid, the realisation that his partner had just closed a work placement for him now dawning on him. The fact he would have done the same as Ramin didn't help. Besides, he had his own shitshow to deal with. Just how did he miss the car?

I kicked my legs out and stared up at the ceiling. Did I say I loved live events? I was a fool. Leading a team of fools. I took a deep breath. Those sorts of thoughts were not only wildly inaccurate, they were also completely unhelpful. Just as I began to regroup, Clio stepped in.

'Neith, you were the closest to the exchange. Replay your footage and we can see what happened.'

I linked my glasses to the projector, and we watched as I walked down the street and into the café with Clio beside me. Ten minutes later Charles walked in, followed by Ramin. Clio then got up and walked towards the loos, then the screen went dead.

'Check the connection?'

'I did. We ran it again, but still nothing.'

Clio looked at me and asked calmly when I had last had my equipment serviced. It was a valid question, as I could sometimes be slow to keep everything shipshape. But never on a mission.

'Ramin, run your footage.' We watched as he and Paul parted ways in the street and Ramin followed the dealer into the café. Charles was sitting to the right and Clio and I were sitting to the left. As he walked past us, the screen went dead.

'Clio, Paul, your footage please.' My voice was calm, my body still, but inside I was screaming. Clio's footage traced mine as we walked into the café. We watched

Ramin walk in, then watched as he walked past us. Her screen went black and then flicked on again as Ramin headed to the counter, and a few minutes later she walked out to the toilets, muttering to me that she was in position.

'Paul, yours please.'

Paul arrived with Ramin and stayed in the street, walking up both sides in a standard reconnaissance pattern. Just as it was at the furthest end of the street, tyres could be heard, and he turned and started to run towards the café. The car stopped and two men jumped out and started shooting at the window. One of them then stepped through the broken window and bent down. I could be seen shooting the first man and then stabbing him. Neither action had any significant effect. Climbing back into the car, they had a bag in their hands. The car then drove past Paul and he continued towards the café.

'Okay, Clio, run copies and back-ups of all four pieces of footage. I want to study all of them and try to understand what happened to mine and Ramin's.'

'There was a tiny flicker on Clio's footage at the same time that ours went out,' said Ramin.

'Do you think someone jammed our signal?' asked Paul. It seemed farfetched. But before I could say anything, Clio jumped in.

'Unlikely. For that to be the case, a few other things would need to be established. Someone on Beta Earth shares our technology. Which they don't. Or that someone else from Alpha Earth is over here at the same time. Which they aren't. I can't say for certain, but my best guess at this stage is that my equipment had a surge-fail-recover incident that knocked out all nearby recording technology,' she said, then turned to me. 'I'll run over the equipment later, but I think that is the most obvious explanation.'

I wanted to agree, but it seemed a massive coincidence. The idea of there being a second team running around that I didn't know about was not pleasant, but there was another explanation I wasn't prepared to entertain. We might have an enemy within.

'Okay, Clio, do that after the briefing, and I know no one wants to consider that there's a second team in the field that we're unaware of, but I want us now to all behave as though there is one.' I took a deep breath. 'Right, my verbal report as team leader of the incident.'

I tried to give a full report of everything I could see. It was tedious, but without the actual footage, I needed to be as thorough as possible. I surged on.

'Within a few minutes of the dealer receiving his drink, Charles leant under the table and pulled the bag up from the floor and placed it on his lap. He opened the bag and pulled out a wooden matryoshka doll. It was painted in a naïve Russian folk art style from the early twentieth century. It was approximately eight inches tall and five inches wide at its widest point, tapering down to approximately three inches wide, top and bottom.'

I motioned the approximate size with my hands, and also took a moment to catch a breath.

'The dealer leant forward to touch it, but Charles removed it and placed it back in the bag and put the bag back on the floor between his feet so that he remained in constant contact with the bag. Charles then put his hand in his pocket and put his fist on the table. Both men leant forward as Charles opened his palm. At that point, the other man started laughing. Charles then placed whatever was in his hand back in his pocket. The two men now started to talk rapidly as a car pulled up and the shooting began.'

'What was in his hand? Did you see?'

'No, but I did manage to pick his pocket.' Out of my own pocket I now pulled an opaque plexiform box. Opening it up, I carefully picked out a little figurine of a boy carved in ruby. We all sighed in appreciation of the pure artistry of the little model, only slightly larger than a thumbnail.

'So, they have the egg,' Paul said, interrupting my report. 'Great Ra! We may as well step back and face the music then.' The three of us stared at him.

'Have you lost your marbles?' Ramin said. 'This is a live event. We don't step back until the dead date has passed. We still have every chance of recovering the egg.' Ramin was cross that his partner was so rattled. Looking at me, he suggested we took a quick break. He had a point. At the moment we had more questions than answers, and at the moment I didn't want to think about what those answers implied.

'Right. Clio, find out what in the name of Ra happened to the recording devices. Paul, trace the car and get visuals on the occupants when they ditched it. Go and talk to anyone in the area. Let's see if we can follow that lead. Ramin, help him with that but don't leave the hotel. I need you to lie low for a while. Check all the CCTV footage and see what the police reports are saying. I'm going to Cambridge to Charles' house tomorrow morning to see if I can find any clues there. When you're done here, I want you ready to relocate to Cambridge. It's time to move operations. We missed our chance here. Now it's time for the endgame.'

#15 Neith – Beta Earth

As I stepped off the train, I headed towards Charles' home. He lived on the other side of the town, so I walked through the heart of Cambridge. I loved Cambridge and Oxford; as with Alpha, these two university towns had developed along similar lines. If anything, the glories of the two Beta towns were stronger and more intense. Possibly because they were such rare examples of collegiate learning.

On Alpha, we had many more examples in every country. Towns that built up around the university colleges, their lineage running back hundreds of years. Some were marking their first millennium. I would never argue less is more when it came to centres of learning and education, but when a civilisation only had a few universities, they became incredible centres of excellence. All the expertise and resources were refined into only a few institutions. It was hardly fair or equitable for the masses, but it did result in towns of deep beauty and focussed learning.

Cambridge was humming, and for the first time on Beta, I felt a little bit more comfortable. There was something in the air that felt like home. Obviously, it wasn't the cold or the drizzle, but here in Cambridge I could ignore all that and I smiled as I headed toward the dead man's house.

I knew that the front door was likely to be watched, so I headed around the back. I had a cloak with me, but I suspected it wouldn't be much use here. Cloaks are good at mirroring, so if you covered yourself in one, people didn't notice you. But it wasn't brilliant; if someone was looking hard they would notice an issue or if they were standing too close, then they would be part of the mirror. It was a bit like a fake moustache; it sort of worked, but for heaven's sake don't rely on it.

Charles' house was bound to be under scrutiny by the neighbours, so they'd notice anything odd. Instead, I was just going to have to rely on good old counter-surveillance skills. Happily, I aced my East Berlin term as well as my Chairman Mao term. And Gaddafi's secret police. Wherever there was fear and suspicion, you could usually find an Alexandrian student trying to get through their exams. And like I said, I aced them. Avoiding detection by a bunch of British suburban neighbours was tricky, but I was up to the task. I left a little wow bang in the bins at the other end of the alley. I loved those little bangs. Packed with psychedelic substances, they moved via air and direct contact dispersal and could trick nearby citizens into thinking or feeling whatever we needed. As it went off, I slipped in through the rear gate and picked the back door's lock.

Inside the house, I discovered it was the abode of a man that didn't live there on a regular basis. The kitchen was spotless, and the fridge only had a few items inside. The freezer was full of frozen ready meals and I imagined the microwave saw the most action in this room. A single coffee cup sat in the sink, waiting to be washed. I swabbed it for DNA just in case it threw up a new lead, but it was unlikely. From the kitchen, I headed into a cluttered room, which was being used as a study. Every wall was covered in bookshelves and there was a space for a computer. No doubt the police had impounded it. Annoying, but not unsurprising. He travelled a lot, so he was bound to have a small laptop or tablet somewhere. With any luck, I might find that. He must store his research somewhere, as he was stingy about loading text or backing up his work on the cloud.

This room was in the middle of the house, so the only window overlooked the back yard. Boy, was he paranoid! There was also a pile of sand on the desk. Fingers had run through it, so no doubt the police had checked it and moved on. I dismissed it and carried on looking around the ground floor, careful to avoid the windows.

Climbing the stairs, I saw a few framed photos and some nice pieces of artwork. Very nice in fact, and all originals. This guy had a good eye and I approved of his choices. I ran a thorough check of the bedrooms and bathroom, but drew a blank and headed back downstairs.

A key clicked in the front door. I cursed. I wouldn't be able to get downstairs and out the back door in time; there was a clear view from the front door to the foot of the stairs. Instead, I moved back up, searching for a place to hide.

The front door opened and closed, but only a few seconds later there was a knock and I could hear someone open the door again and a muffled conversation taking place. Nosey neighbour for the win. From the tone of the conversation, the neighbour seemed okay with whoever had opened the door, and there was a low-level hubbub of polite condolences. I held my breath; this was probably going to work out fine. Whoever had just entered the house was obviously a friend or colleague, and they weren't here to search the premises, just switch off the water.

I looked out the back window. I might be able to climb out and escape back along the alleyway. My gut clenched though when I saw two men at the far end of the alley. I had a bad feeling that they weren't coming to water the plants.

#16 Julius – Beta Earth

With Charlie's spare keys safely pocketed, Julius cycled back into town.

The shock of hearing of his friend's death was still overwhelming him. He paused to consider Charlie's parents, career diplomats currently living in the US. He would need to get in touch with them to offer his condolences. They were nice people, and he'd enjoyed staying at their house during school holidays. They used to ask him constantly if he was alright because they weren't used to such a quiet boy. He wasn't looking forward to the next time he met them. He couldn't believe that only a few days ago he and Charlie had been laughing and speculating about what finding a Fabergé egg would mean. Wealth, fame, glory. Neither, for a minute, had considered death. With those thoughts came pain and isolation and fear. Julius wiped a tear away as he continued to pedal into town. There was no point in being maudlin. That wasn't going to solve anything.

He propped up his bike in Charlie's small front garden and opened the door. Charlie's house was a typical Cambridge terrace. The front door opened into a welcoming front room, and beyond that, separated by the staircase, was a dining room he used as a study and then through to the kitchen. Everything was on display. His friend's home was an open book, unlike his life. He looked at the sofa where he and Charlie would sit and play on the Xbox until dawn, killing zombies and aliens, drinking beers, and putting the world to rights. Julius preferred Assassin's Creed and Charlie always thrashed him at it, but that wasn't the point. Just hanging out with his friend had been the point.

Julius took a deep breath. If he were going to find any clues to his friend's murder, it would be in the study.

A knock on the front door caught him unawares and he jumped. The police would no doubt have already visited, and the killers were unlikely to knock. Feeling both foolish and nervous, he answered the door, only to see Charlie's next-door neighbour standing in front of him.

Mrs Mack was an older woman who lived for her own opinions, and the lives, but not the opinions, of her neighbours. There wasn't a soul who twitched on this street that Mrs Mack didn't know about.

'Oh, Julius, it's you. I didn't know who it was. I thought the killers may be back.'

'They were never here, Mrs Mack.'

'Such terrible news. I haven't been able to sleep. The police won't be able to catch them. Foreigners I hear.'

'I don't think the police have released any information—'

'Oh yes, well no doubt they've spoken to you as well. They spoke to me, they wanted to know if I had seen anything. I told them. I showed them my notebooks.'

Julius looked at her, appalled. Did she actually keep records on the comings and goings of her neighbours? How many times did he feature?

'And were you able to help them?'

Mrs Mack went on to explain how she offered them valuable information on the council binmen who she thought were illegal aliens, and the postman who may be stealing, and the couple down the street who were fiddling their benefits. Mrs Mack lived in a world of crime and fear. Ironically, the one time that something truly fearful happened, she had no information or sightings. She had seen no one visit Charlie's home other than Charlie, and there'd been no strange cars parked on the street or anything else unusual.

Julius thanked her for her unoffered condolences and excused himself, saying he needed to take care of things. Mrs Mack offered to help, but the idea of her stepping into Charlie's house filled him with revulsion; she was already peering over his shoulder, eager to snoop into Charlie's private life.

Closing the door, he leant against it and took a deep breath. This wasn't helping. He walked into the study and looked around. The computer was gone, but he assumed the police would have taken that. His phone would have been on him, but he wondered if they had also taken his tablet. There were a few postcards and photos up on a pinboard. Above the desk the pinboard was covered in more work-related items: images of stacking dolls, Fabergé artwork, and news clippings

116

about the Russian revolution. This was clearly the current project, but then, Julius knew all this already. The only thing that was catching his eye was a pile of sand on the side table. Fingers had trailed tracks through it. He sat down and studied the sand. That was completely out of place. Pausing to think, he studied the bookshelves. Charlie had lined this room with them, while the paintings had been relegated to the staircase and bedrooms. The shelves didn't only house books, but mementoes that had been collected on his travels. There were spears, spent tank shells, and carriage clocks.

He laughed when he remembered one of the clocks. Charlie had got a real bee in his bonnet about it. He was convinced it was a rare early example of a particular French clockmaker. He had found it during a house clearance in Ireland. At the bottom of the clock face was a very unusual date and maker's mark. "Oth. 1.1.66" rather than the more usual "January 1st, 1866". Something about the date rang alarm bells for Julius, and he warned Charlie to not pay over the odds. Charlie bought it anyway, as he had never seen dating like that before and thought it might be very rare. A few days later Julius remembered the old diaries he'd been reading by a travelling curate. The curate remarked on a clever set of forgeries he had seen a local metal worker making. He was making carriage clocks in the style of a well-known Frenchman. The curate had not approved of the deception but admired the artistry, and had told

117

the forger to engrave his clocks with a warning, "1.1.66". The metalworker had, but few knew their Shakespeare well enough and the warning became a clue too well hidden.

So, whilst Charlie had paid a decent price for an undiscovered early carriage clock in the French style, he had paid grossly over the odds for a forgery. In the end, he kept it. Julius felt his friend could have made some money back on it, with the provenance that he had dug up, but Charlie was determined. He enjoyed the fact that he had run after something that had glittered and ignored his friend's warning. After that, he generally phoned Julius before making an expensive purchase, just in case it rang more alarm bells.

Julius continued to look along the shelves at some of those items. A few were certainly collectable, or even valuable, but most were just mementoes of a trip or a person. Nor was there any particular theme: fossils, vases, wooden boxes, an ivory totem, a carved glass bust, and there, in the corner, an old wooden stacking doll. That was new. And Russian.

As he reached towards it, he heard a small creak from an upstairs floorboard. He recognised that sound. Whenever he slept over following a late night, he would stay in the back room and would creak out of bed.

Julius wouldn't call himself brave, and right now he would go with pissed off. If someone were hiding upstairs, then they were simply being rude. Part of his mind was screaming that this wasn't the time to get in a twist over good manners, but this was Charlie's home and Charlie had been murdered. It just wasn't on for someone to skulk around upstairs.

He headed up the staircase, calling out, but heard nothing. Walking into the back bedroom, he saw a small woman crouched down peeking out over the sill of the window.

'Who the hell…'

She turned and looked at him, gesturing wildly. 'Get down, you idiot!'

'I beg your—'

'Now!' she hissed with the full force of a command. She was small and wiry, with straight black hair. At a guess, he would say she was southern Mediterranean, and possibly pretty if she wasn't quite so intimidating. It wasn't that intimidating people couldn't be good-looking, it was just not very high on his list of priorities.

Julius paused and crouched down, then crawled over to her. Peering over the sill, he saw two men in the back courtyard. One tried the handle of the back door, and when it wouldn't give, he took off his jacket and placed it against the glass pane, then broke it. Leaning in, he dropped the deadbolt and opened the door.

'I'll call the police,'

The strange woman stared at Julius as if he were an idiot and put her finger on his lips. Taking the phone from his hand, she switched it to mute and put it back in his pocket.

'I need you to stay very still and silent,' she whispered. 'Things are about to get very scary. Tuck yourself into that corner.'

Julius looked to where she gestured and shook his head. She gave him a small shove, and he hissed back. 'The floorboard squeaks.'

The woman tipped her head, then cracked a small smile and rolled her eyes. 'Okay, stay here and stay quiet.'

She edged to the bedroom door and listened to the men below. Julius followed her to listen as well, earning a massive glare and some arm-waving gestures. He ignored her and continued to listen to the conversation below.

'How the fuck should I know where it is? All she said was look out for a jewelled egg. It'll be about this big. You check the fridge. I'll do the cupboards.'

Julius listened in outrage as drawers and doors were opened and closed and things fell on the floor. The woman placed a warning hand on his knee.

'Right, let's try in here. I don't want to be the one to tell her we failed.'

'Jesus, look at all this crap. I bet one of these books has a secret compartment. Come on, let's do this.'

A large book thudded onto the floor and Julius flinched, then stood up.

'Get down,' hissed the woman, 'I've got this.' She threw a small round object the size of a conker down the stairs. Turning, she grabbed Julius' arm and squeezed it. 'Get back! This is going to be unpleasant. Close your eyes and block your nose. If you can also block your ears that will help. It won't last long. Remember that everything you see is a hallucination.'

She pulled him away from the top of the stairs, back towards the rear window, just as he heard one of the men shout out in alarm. As she went to watch from the window, he was about to ask what she thought she was doing when he heard screams of pure terror from downstairs, followed by a foul smell that wafted up the stairs to him. It was the smell of abattoirs and rotting meat, fear and blood and excrement, and something decomposing underneath that made him want to gag. The air around him became chilly, and suddenly the very marrow of his bones froze as a wave of primordial revulsion raced across his skin. Looking down, he saw wet fingers wrap themselves around his ankle. He shrieked in alarm. The strange woman by the window hurried toward him as a monstrous creature coalesced from the ceiling, its abnormally wide mouth opening wider and wider, saliva dripping from its teeth and ready to bite him in half.

'Block your ears and close your eyes,' she said as she pinched his nose. Instantly, the room warmed up and fell silent. He was sitting on a carpet, and apart from the strange woman, nothing else was touching him. He opened his eyes and saw the walls dripping with black ooze. His body juddered, and she turned away from the window and tapped his eyes with her free hand. He clamped them shut again.

What the hell was going on? He was switching between full-on panic and mild annoyance. Of the two, he preferred peeved and sat in silence like the proverbial monkey. Then, just as he was wondering how long this would last, she let go of his nose and gently removed his hands from his ears. Opening his eyes, he saw her face was awfully close to his. She was smiling.

'Okay?'

He cautiously looked around the room. There was no monster on the ceiling ready to eat someone, and the walls were free of arms trying to tear the skin from his limbs. The air smelled of Charlie's aftershave and carpet dust. The house was silent.

'What the hell just happened?'

'Wow bang. Clever little device, designed to get rid of bad people. Some make noises, others make monsters.'

'How did you know they were bad people?'

'You mean, besides them throwing a book on the floor?'

'Well, yes, obviously they'd marked their card at that point. But you were already treating them as the bad guys.'

'Only bad guys break in through the back door.'

She had a point. He would expect the police to knock on the front door, or anyone else for that matter.

She was right, only people up to no good came in through the back door.

'How did you get in here by the way?'

'I picked the lock and came in through the back door.'

He paused and looked at her as she left the window and headed downstairs, ignoring him.

'Hang on!'

In the study, she had already picked up the book and put it back on the bookshelf, and now was tiding up the other objects that had been moved around. Picking up the set of wooden dolls, she opened up the first one and looked inside.

'How long has he had this?'

Julius was about to reply when the events of the last ten minutes finally caught up with him.

'Who the hell are you? And put that down.'

The woman put the doll down and held out her hand. 'I'm Neith, and I'm trying to find out why your friend was killed.'

Julius was reluctant to shake this strange woman's hand, as memories of dead limbs seeping through the wallpaper to grab at him still lingered. Still, an outstretched hand was hard to refuse, so he leant forward. 'Are you the police then?'

'A special branch of them, yes. We believe your friend was killed for something he had just found. Something that he may have brought back from Poland. Oh, you've got something on your nose.'

She swiped the side of her nose with her fingers, and he followed suit. 'All gone,' she said and smiled. 'You were saying?'

Julius suddenly felt an overwhelming compulsion to talk. 'No, the dolls were just a clue. They tipped off Charlie to the idea that he might be on the track of a Fabergé egg.' He paused. Why the hell was he telling her all this?

'I am with the police, remember?'

He stared at her and shook his head. 'Yes, sorry about that. So anyway, he flew back to England and asked me to research the family. Sure enough, there was a strong connection to early twentieth-century Russia. And I found the man's brother living in London. Charlie called me last week. He had the egg and had it hidden all these years in the large outer doll. I think that's what this sand is. I think the sand cushioned the egg in the doll.'

'Did he tell you what he did with the egg itself?'

'I assume he took it to the meeting?'

'No, obviously not. Look, I've added my number to your phone. Call me if you think of anything. Make yourself a coffee and stay away from men with guns.'

Standing up, she gave him a small bow and then headed out the back door. Julius looked after her, perplexed. Something was wrong, but he wasn't quite sure what it was. He had a strong urge for a cup of coffee, so he flicked on the kettle and began to tidy up the kitchen. After one sip of coffee, he shot out the back door, hoping to catch sight of which way the strange woman had gone. What the hell was wrong with him? He had blurted out all that stuff about the egg without so much as asking to see her ID card. If she was the police, why did she break in? And why did she leave so quickly?

Angry with himself, he tried to replay the past half hour, but it seemed ridiculous. Monsters and burglars? Verbal diarrhoea and strange women? And no egg. He tried to remember what she had said. "It was obvious that they didn't have the egg?" Why? He took another sip and chided himself for his stupidity. If they had the egg, they wouldn't have broken in looking for it. What else did she say? He pulled out his phone and opened his contacts, scrolling to the Ns and hit dial. She answered after the first ring.

'Hello, Julius. Have you had any coffee?'

'Yes, but what's that got to do with anything. I want—'

'Good. Now, like I said, call me if anything new happens. You did really well today. Goodbye.'

'I'm going to call the police!'

'Okay. Goodbye.' This time she hung up.

He dialled again, but the phone went straight to voicemail. Picking up the nested Russian dolls, he placed them in his backpack and cycled straight to the police station.

The police officers took his statement and looked at the dolls with mild interest, then said they would send officers to investigate the house again. The idea that a Fabergé egg may be involved had piqued their interest, and they said that the London detectives were sure to get in touch soon. For some reason he hadn't mentioned Neith; he had felt a strange sense of gratitude to her for helping him out, plus he felt they had bonded over their mutual annoyance at the books being thrown about. If he was honest, he felt that if he had to explain her presence, he would also have to explain the weird visions and the fact that he blabbed his mouth off to a total stranger. He'd had enough of acting like a total idiot for the day, and he didn't want to be sectioned for the evening.

He left the station deflated; the officers hadn't even asked to keep the doll, so he cycled home and placed it on his mantelpiece, then poured himself a large glass of red wine. His head ached and he just wanted Charlie to be alive.

#17 Neith – Beta Earth

The weather was miserable. Something cold fell from the sky, and it was either wet snow or fat raindrops. I hurried back to our house. The heating pads on my base layer had worn out and I was shivering badly. I know I'm supposed to be stronger than this, and I am. I have spent hours holed up in snowdrifts above Uppsala. I even trudged through the Siberian tundra in November. I can do cold. But there's something about the damp wet sludge of the British mainland in winter that just destroys me. I'd only been here a fortnight, but I was already missing the baking mud of the banks of the Canopus, the light breezes by the Saharan oasis. Hell, I'd been homesick since day one.

I pulled my phone out of my padded jacket pocket and called Clio. We needed to know everything about Charles' friends, in particular, who had access to his house keys. Before I hung up, I told her to run a hot bath, then continued along the street. My hood was up, and I was hunkered down against the elements and the general population. The man I'd met had been interesting. Betas never attracted me much. I mean, don't get me wrong, my blood runs red and he was unbelievably hot. But what I meant was that he had caught my attention. Despite the horrors of the psychedelic bang, he had managed to not soil his pants, which was more than we could say about the two goons who had been downstairs. He'd done some pretty impressive research, and I liked his theory about the sand. Brave and intelligent beats pretty, any day.

The egg was somewhere here in Cambridge, I was certain of it. In three days it would surface, as it rolled out of someone's hand and under the path of a double-decker bus.

We had booked a private house rather than a hotel. In a small city like Cambridge, this gave us greater privacy. Hotels here were too intimate and we would draw attention to ourselves. Instead, I hurried back to our city-centre house and ran up the staircase and into the bathroom, shedding my layers as I went. I shouted out to the team that we would debrief in the bathroom.

The room was steamy, and from the smell, Clio had poured half a box of aromatic salts into the water. Peeling off my bottom layer, I slipped into the water and let out a deep, contented sigh.

'Shall I join you?' said a grinning Ramin as he walked in with the others.

'Bugger off. There's barely room in here for one and I am not sharing.'

Paul had booked the best he could, but the only ones with steam rooms or saunas were miles out in the countryside, so baths it was. And this small one was mine. The British on either earth were not fans of communal bathing, so they built their baths for one. Occasionally, a second person would join the bath for some physical recreation. Which was ludicrous. The bath was only built for one, and even then a lot of their baths were almost too small for a single person. Maybe the British do it differently? Either way, their baths are certainly not big enough to share and chat in. The three brought in chairs and I began by telling them all that had happened.

'Okay,' began Clio, 'I think the guy you encountered in the upstairs bedroom is called Julius Strathclyde.'

'Julius? Good grief! What's wrong with his parents? Sorry, continue.' It was irrational of me; Adolf and Hitler were perfectly bland names over on Alpha but here on Beta you'd have to wonder about why someone would name their child that. That's how we feel about Julius back home; burning down our library made us twitchy like that.

'He went to school with Charles. Calls him Charlie. They have kept in touch ever since. The probability is extremely high that this is the only person with a spare key to his house. Neither man has a large social media footprint. In fact, they are positively antiquarian. It's frustrating, actually. If you need to know more about this guy, I'm going to have to do some legwork. He's a professor in ancient languages and religions. And it seems that as a part-time activity he volunteers as an archivist for the Fitzwilliam Museum.'

'I knew I had a good feeling about him. Did I mention he held his nerve during a psychedelic wow bang?'

The three of them nodded appreciatively.

'Why didn't you get more information from him directly? You had time, right?' asked Ramin.

I sank under the water and came up again. I was still cold. 'Did you run this bath with cold water mixed in?' Running the hot water tap, I carried on. 'He was very resistant. I would class him as both highly intelligent and moral.'

'Bugger,' said Paul. 'Did you get anything at all?'

'He knows about the egg, but he doesn't know where it is, and I don't believe he has anything to do with the people that murdered his friend or are after the egg.'

'How did you apply the truth serum?'

'Handshake.'

'And?'

'And he paused when I questioned him.'

'Damn! He actively resisted you, even after you applied the drug?' asked Clio. 'Did you —'

'Yes, I got him to inhale it the usual way. I got him to touch his nose. At that point, he answered, but he was hugely reluctant. I was concerned that he would break out.'

That was the problem with moral and intelligent, you could only lead them in the direction they wanted to go as there was nothing duplicitous in them. The other difficult personality set was the immoral, intelligent ones because they invariably would lead you wherever they wanted to go. In our line of work we regularly came across both sets. Thieves and geniuses have lots in common. And then of course there's us, the curators. Intelligence is a prerequisite, morals aren't. And of course, morals didn't always have to comply with societal norms. A person with a strong moral code does not automatically obey the law. In fact, the more intelligent they were the more often they deferred to their own moral standards than those of society's. Happily, though, they tended to run along the same course. Otherwise, you'd be overrun with vigilantes.

'Why didn't you just force the answers?'

'Because I think we need him.'

'Was he very good looking?' Clio asked in a coy voice.

I laughed and splashed water at her. 'Idiot. Paul, pass me a gown, I don't want to freeze to death. Let's continue this in front of the fire.' One of the major pluses of a house rather than a hotel.

Settling down in the living room, I caught up on what the others had to report.

'I haven't heard any rumours about the egg,' Ramin said. 'Charles made no mention of it anywhere on his phone or social media, neither did the dealer. We can't even be certain that's why they met, except that the doll case he briefly put on the table fits in with the story Julius told you about.' Ramin put another log on the fire and continued while Paul made us some hot chocolates. That's something the northern countries excelled in, and if I drank too many more I'd have to add a few miles to my daily run.

'I think we can also assume the egg wasn't in the doll case.'

'How can we be certain?' asked Paul.

Clio rolled her eyes. 'They already have the outer doll case. Why would they have broken into his house if they had the egg, stupid.'

'Okay, concentrate people, this isn't helping. The egg will resurface. That isn't a problem. What is a problem, is how that car evaded your observance, Paul, and why we haven't been able to track the assailants or their car. London is full of cameras and we have access to all of them. Clio, why don't we know who they are?'

Clio glared and then bit off her reply. We might be best friends, but I was her lead officer on this, and she was failing.

'Honestly, Neith, I don't have a sodding clue. It's as if they knew how to evade every camera. Or they had jammers?'

'Beta technology doesn't have jammers that fine-tuned yet. See if you can spot any anomalies, and trace those instead. Sudden electricity shortages, EM pulses, any Beta technology at the moment will leave a dirty trace. Find that instead.'

'Are we going to consider that it's Alpha technology?' asked Ramin.

We all paused. Obviously, there was a total technology embargo, but it wasn't impossible that something had been left behind, either lost or forgotten. But then they'd have to know how to use them, and most Alpha technology was biometrically driven.

'Come on, Ramin. I think we can rule that scenario out. I can entertain the idea of there being a second team here, but not one that's working against us?'

'Fair enough,' he said and shrugged. 'I just think we need to be open to any variable. As you say, this doesn't make sense. Also, who's the woman the two men referred to at Charles' house?'

Paul read his notes. '*Fucking mad bitch*. Either of you two want to volunteer for the position?'

Clio and I laughed. It was an epitaph we had heard many times, on many missions.

'Whose turn is it this month, yours or mine?' asked Clio.

The hot chocolate and crackling logs were finally warming me up, and despite the urgency and the issues, I was enjoying myself. These three people were my best friends, and I was safe and happy. The job was properly stretching me, and the company was excellent. Life was good.

'Alright. Paul and Clio, a bit of legwork for you. There's a memorial service for Charles coming up, so please can you check out the venue? Julius is likely to be there. I think he's now the key to finding the egg early. I don't want another attack. Ramin, can you dig deep and see what you can find out about him? I suggest you go to his place of work, as he hasn't left much of a digital footprint. Talk to people, see what they say.'

'And what are you going to do?'

'Research the egg. Here, by the fire. I'll even cook dinner.'

Laughing, we broke up. My culinary skills extended to ordering takeaways. Fish and chips for four.

#18 Julius – Beta Earth

Julius went over his notes for the eulogy and then, utterly deflated, he pushed away his laptop and made himself an omelette. He was exhausted and hadn't been able to shake his headache. He knew this was partly grief, but he still couldn't get over the events of the previous afternoon and the strange woman in Charlie's house. She had been wearing black jeans, fur-trimmed leather boots and a dark, slim-fitting jumper. With her blunt bob and heavy-framed glasses, she looked like any student you would find in Cambridge. But Julius was convinced no one would ever mistake her for a student, not if they looked closely.

He wasn't sure what he thought she was, but the way she'd ignored him and taken control made him think military. The more he thought about her story, the less he thought she was police as she had claimed. She was entirely too self-controlled. Was she also after the egg? He didn't think she was involved in the shooting. After all, she had saved him from the men who had broken into Charlie's. And what was that thing that she had thrown down the stairs? Some sort of hallucinogenic nerve agent? Whatever it was, he wouldn't be surprised if those two were now under psychiatric care. The tiny dose he had experienced had been terrifying, and she had shown him how to protect himself. He supposed it was relief that had made him gabble like a school child.

But at least she seemed interested in what he had to say, whilst the police had almost yawned.

He looked at his watch and saw that he had lost track of time. Realising the moment had come, he scraped his cold, uneaten omelette into the bin and set off to Charlie's memorial service.

The church was packed with Charlie's friends, family and colleagues. He had been a popular fellow, but few could say they knew him well. That wasn't his style; he travelled too much to settle down and build close relationships. Besides his parents, Julius was the only other person in the congregation that could claim to properly know Charlie. Despite that, there were many sad faces and tears. He was, after all, popular. And if you had asked anyone in the room, they would have all claimed to be a close personal friend. Julius stood beside Charlie's bewildered parents.

They had spoken privately earlier and already knew of his involvement in the emergence of a possible Fabergé egg. It didn't help much, but at least it explained his violent death. The fact that his death had been instantaneous and in the middle of him doing something he loved, was the tiniest of consolations. It was all they could hang on to right now. If only for them, Julius wanted to find the egg. Maybe he could donate it to the museum in Charlie's name?

Walking up to the lectern, he gazed over the congregation. He had never enjoyed being the centre of attention. When he gave a lecture, he expected the students to pay attention to the message, not the messenger.

He decided to start the eulogy this way, explaining that he was pretending this was a lecture and he was going to tell them about a most fascinating subject. The congregation gave bittersweet chuckles. He didn't need notes as his memory was perfect, and talking about Charlie was never a challenge. He just wished he was in the congregation, yawning loudly at him and gesturing that they bugger off early and get a pint.

Looking out over the faces, he saw two men enter the back of the church. Julius didn't recognise them. They certainly didn't look like academics, more like the heavy mob. The men fanned out on either side of the church and began to walk down the side of the pews. Julius carried on speaking but was distracted by a second group of people entering the church. This time there were four of them and one of them at least was familiar. The smaller of the two women was the one he had met in Charlie's house. He stumbled, and she looked over at him, giving him a little thumbs up, then continued to follow one of the first men around the edge of the congregation.

As Julius faltered, one of the first men turned his head to see what he was staring at. As soon as the thug saw that someone had followed him into the church, he paused. Julius paused too, unsure of what was happening. He looked at Neith, who shrugged and smiled, then leant against the wall of the church.

Clearing his throat, Julius continued, a rush of anger taking him through his final thoughts. How dare these people intrude on Charlie's final moments. Gripping the lectern, he brought the speech to an end and walked down the aisle and out into the churchyard. Convention be damned. He had no desire to stay for the rest of the service, nor engage in small talk afterwards. He was also uncertain what the presence of the strangers indicated, and he had no desire to find out. He was angry, and he needed to walk it off.

Outside the sun was shining and the street beyond was quiet. It seemed mad that the world just continued on whilst his life seemed in utter disarray. He knew that was just life, but he was jumping at shadows and sleeping badly.

He had almost made it to the lychgate when two men approached him from the street. They looked like the two thugs who had come into the church first. He chided himself for not being alert, but just as he was about to politely smile at them, one of them stepped forward and grabbed his arm. Angry, and feeling foolish, he took a deep breath to shout out when a rough hand clamped over his mouth. These guys weren't playing, and he slumped like a dead weight to destabilise them. As one of them stumbled, he shoved at him and was gratified as he lost his grip on Julius' arm. Struggling with the other assailant, he realised other people had joined the fray. As far as he could work out, it was the two thugs from the church and the four who had followed them in.

He looked over at the church, but the door was closed so no one else from the eulogy would be coming to join in the fight. Within seconds, the scene was chaotic. He paused as a tall and utterly stunning woman ran towards him and then kicked him in the belly. He doubled over, falling to his knees, though as he did so he felt something pass overhead. Fights were breaking out all around him. The woman who had kicked him grabbed him by the arm and started calling his name. He didn't think he could breathe. The pain in his stomach was immense, and he thought he was going to be sick; this was worse than rugby. She grabbed his arm again and then stood up, punching a man in the throat who ran towards them.

'Get in the fucking car! Ramin, help me carry him.'

That was enough for Julius. No one was going to carry him. He tried to stand up but was still heavily winded. The other woman, Neith, was spinning and kicking, fighting against two men. Beside her, a huge beast of a man covered in tattoos and bad life choices was trading blows with one of the two men who'd entered the church. She glanced over briefly and grinned, giving him another thumbs up. That decided it. She appeared to approve of the two people now trying to get him to a car. He stumbled along with them and was all but thrown into the backseat whilst his two rescuers jumped into the front seats and sped off.

He stared out the back window, trying to make sense of what had just happened. The congregation was still safely ensconced within the church whilst the fight continued amongst the gravestones. As his eyes followed Neith in admiration, a man crept up behind her. He tried to wave at her and alert her to the danger, but she simply waved back as the man punched the back of her head.

Julius watched in horror as she collapsed in a heap.

#19 Neith – Beta Earth

Looking back, I knew it was all going to go belly up when I flicked Julius a thumbs up in the church. Nothing good ever came of churches. This was proving to be no exception. A thumbs up, like a stupid kid. I deserved all I got.

The day had started better. Ramin had spent the previous day at the museum and library, posing in turns as a visiting academic, a reporter, even an undergrad. Every time he spoke to someone, the topic would weave back to Charles or Julius, as though it were the speaker themself who introduced the topic. It was always the best sort of interrogation technique, as the blabbermouth would be slow to reveal, if later questioned, that they had raised the topic of conversation.

Talking to people and getting them to relax in his company was a particular skill of Ramin's. He might go toe to toe with Clio when it came to paper and internet research skills, but when it came to humans, he was ahead by a country mile. I reckon it's because he liked people and Clio didn't. Clio has never been what you could call a people person.

He'd discovered that someone else had been asking about Julius and Charles. This wasn't good. We still didn't have a clear idea of who our opponents were.

Normally it was your local bad guys or meddling do-gooders. The former camp was easier to deal with, in that we didn't need to worry about hurting their feelings, or their persons for that matter. I mean, no one dies. Well, rarely, well apart from Napoleon, but that wasn't our fault. Well, not absolutely, but I wasn't on that team anyway, so absolutely not my fault. For once.

So, sometimes people die. The ones we try not to have die are the good-willed meddlers. Like Charles, the dealer and Julius. Two out of three was not a good strike rate. The death of the old Polish lady also seemed suspicious. I didn't like the idea of losing another innocent party, especially a fellow curator. His looks had nothing to do with it. Honestly, at that point, so far I had seen his angry face, his scared face, his worried face and his bloody terrified face, but not his happy or relaxed faces. It's hard to judge someone's appearance when they are trying to assess how dangerous you are. Although I have to admit, I do admire a man who is such a quick and accurate judge of character.

And now someone was after him.

'So, where's the memorial?' asked Clio.

'St Bernardus. Eleven am. I think we need to stake the place out. I also think there's a problem with Julius. Someone's following him. Other than us, I mean. If we're on the ground and we can save him some unnecessary torture, then I say we should be the cowboys,' I replied.

'The cowboys were responsible for the attempted genocide of the native American race,' Clio drawled.

'Oh, I always get that the wrong way around. We be the injuns, then.'

Now Clio was openly laughing at me. 'But the Native American Indians were responsible for the slaughter of thousands of innocent women and children settlers.'

I shrugged my shoulders and smiled. 'We be the curators?'

The other three responded with the time-honoured refrain, 'We preserve!' And chinking our beer glasses we started to wind down for the evening.

The following morning we had taken up our places around the church. Clio thought this was overkill and had been suggesting that, whilst the service was taking place, we search Julius' office and home. She had a point, Paul backed her up, and I was almost convinced, until Ramin asked if I could live with our target being tortured. I agreed with him, despite Clio's annoyance. I loved her dearly, and at times like these she could put me to shame. She was so focussed on the objective, which made her invaluable on the team, but it was my job to focus on the bigger picture, and that included collateral damage.

Sure enough, no sooner had we arrived than I noticed a group of men heading towards the church who did not look like mourners. They didn't look like mourners in the same way that a little old lady doesn't look like a shot-putter. Those black suits weren't fooling anyone. Maybe it was the gun-shaped bulges that were the problem. Guns and churches, that age-old tradition.

We slipped into the church behind them and flanked them on either side. I didn't think they would try to do anything in the church itself. This culture had big taboos about disturbing a religious service. I mean, they were British. There were some places they just didn't kick off. Churches were one, as were opera houses and school assemblies. On the other hand, WI meetings were a positive powder keg and only marginally less flammable than a football stadium. No, for my money they were going to mingle with the mourners, and then quietly grab Julius outside.

As we made our way into the church I could see Julius up at the front talking, and everyone was listening to him attentively. His speech faltered briefly, and I saw him look over at me. I probably shouldn't have done the thumbs up, but he seemed so cross that I just wanted to try giving him some encouragement. On reflection, it could have been my presence that was making him cross.

As he finished speaking, instead of sitting back down he stormed down the aisle. We quickly followed him back out the door and watched in horror as a second team of strangers was already dragging Julius towards a black van.

'Clio, Ramin! Get Julius to the house. Paul, with me!'

The four of us ran forward, all attacking the two men who had Julius, and then Paul and I split off to tackle their reinforcements. Soon it was two on one, hardly a fair fight, and I laughed as I saw Paul spin on one leg under the arm of one thug, whilst his outstretched leg, still spinning, caught the man on the back of his calves and brought him to the ground.

I was similarly engaged. The larger, bulkier men were no match for my small stature and speed. I glanced over to where Julius was standing like an idiot trying to assess the situation. He could have been Nelson surveying a lack of ships. One of the men came charging towards him, and would surely have had him if Clio hadn't also come running, and with a flying kick to his stomach, sent Julius safely out of harm's way. It seemed unclear if he would appreciate her intervention, lying as he was on the ground and gasping for air. I'd remind her later about the appropriate use of force. For now, I gave him a quick salute and watched as Ramin and Clio got him to our car and screeched away.

Thankfully, no one from the church had come out. A lusty rendition of All Things Bright and Beautiful will drown out the loudest of street fights. As I looked at Julius staring out of the back of the car, he seemed to give me a wave and stupidly I waved back. That's when my lights went out.

#20 Julius – Beta Earth

Julius wasn't certain if he had just jumped out of the frying pan and into a steaming pile of dung.

The chap in the front seat turned around to smile at him. 'Put your mind at rest. We're the good guys. I'm Ramin, and this is Clio. Neith and Paul will re-join us soon.'

The foul giver of kicks was driving like Miss Daisy. Having screeched away from the scene, they were now driving sedately through the Cambridge back streets and attracting no attention.

'If Neith is your colleague, I just saw her punched on the back of the head and go down.'

Clio laughed. 'Man, will she be pissed off she let someone get the better of her.'

Ramin seemed less amused. 'Did she get up?'

'Not that I saw. It was quite a blow, but then we flew around the corner and I lost sight of her. I think we should go back.'

Ramin seemed prepared to agree when he touched his earpiece and Clio nodded.

'No, it's okay, that was Paul. They'll be joining us soon. Neith took a blow and Paul fought them off.'

'Paul rescues Neith,' snorted Clio. 'Oh boy, will Neith ever be livid.'

The car pulled up in a wide suburban street and drove onto the large private driveway of an expansive detached Victorian townhouse.

Julius sat in the back of the car, reluctant to leave. Ramin seemed like a good egg, whilst Clio appeared rotten to the core. Ramin followed Julius' expression as she walked to the front door.

'Trust me, mate, she's one of the good guys. Scary as the day is long, but she's on our side. Besides which, she's a pussycat compared to Neith. Now come on. I've got some painkillers for that stomach of yours. Her feet can land quite a blow. She ruptured a man's kidneys once, from the front! Trust me, if she'd wanted to cause you harm, harm she would've caused.'

Julius walked into an upmarket holiday let. Everything was beautifully appointed though there wasn't an ounce of character anywhere. A wall of warm air swept out the front door, and he winced at the obvious waste of energy. He was even more surprised when he saw Clio was lighting a fire in the front room.

He stood in the hallway, uncertain what to do next. Clio was studiously ignoring him and Ramin had wandered off towards the back of the house.

'Come on then,' Ramin said as he reappeared with a small first-aid box. 'Let's go and sit down and see what the damage is.'

Ramin walked into the living room and Julius followed.

'Who were those men in the graveyard and who are you?' Julius asked. 'Neith said she was with the police, but none of you act like policemen.'

Clio looked over. 'Know many policemen, do you?'

'No, it's just. Well, you're not. Are you?'

Neither answered, and Ramin tapped him on the hand to get his attention. 'Lift your shirt and let's see what damage Clio did.'

'That's got to be a record for you, Ramin.'

'Knock it off, Clio, you kicked him pretty hard. I'm just going to fix it.'

'Chill. I was joking. Besides which, shouldn't you be running a bath for Neith?'

Ramin sighed dramatically and then winked at Julius. 'Ignore her. She screwed up the mission. She was in charge of reconnaissance. No way should we have been caught unawares by a second outside team.' He grinned as Clio attacked a log with the poker with more force than was necessary.

'Julius here needs medical attention and Neith would be pissed if she thought we had put her needs ahead of his.'

Clio stood up and went upstairs. 'I'll run the bath then.' As she climbed the staircase, Julius heard her mutter something about *fucking shit flies*.

'Like I said, ignore her. She's also worried about Neith. It's always a worry when you have to leave a team member behind. Those two have been friends since basic training, and teammates as soon as teams were assigned. They are the longest-running partnership in our unit. Come on now, lift your shirt.'

Julius reacted in astonishment as the gel gently warmed his torso and removed all the spasms he had been experiencing. He had been unaware of how hunched over he'd been until he felt his shoulders relax and his body straighten up.

'What is that? Some sort of weapons-grade analgesic?'

'Not analgesic. Well partly, but it's also healing, not just masking. Nifty isn't it? Strictly for missions, but I don't know a single curator that doesn't have a stash at home. Man, it can fix even the worst hangovers.' He pulled Julius' top back down. 'Now what can I get you to drink? Tea, coffee, something stronger?'

With the pain gone, Julius was able to think clearly. 'I've just come from a fight outside the memorial service of my best friend. I don't want a drink, I want answers.'

#21 Neith – Beta Earth

My head hurt and I felt sick. I became aware that I was sitting in a car with Paul driving. I must have groaned, as he pulled over.

'Are you going to be sick?'

I thought about it and tried to shake my head, but that was setting off little earthquakes across my vision. Maybe throwing up was a good idea.

'We'll be home in a second. I'm so sorry, Neith.'

I moved my head slowly to look at Paul. Something in his voice sounded wrong and I was appalled to see tears in his eyes.

'I'm not dead,' I protested, trying to make him laugh. We couldn't be intimate whilst on a mission, but that didn't mean we stopped caring for each other. I knew Paul was struggling with this mission. His failure to spot the car that killed Charles had put a strain on things, but that was work. I didn't want our work relationship to spoil our personal one.

'This is all my fault.' A tear slid down his face, and I suddenly found that I was the one consoling him.

'I think you'll find I was the one that didn't duck in time. Not you. So, what happened after I decided to take a nap?'

Paul wiped the tear away and tried to smile at my weak joke. 'The fight continued for a bit, but as soon as it dawned on them that Julius was safe in the car, they ran off.'

He held my hand for a bit longer, but I must have groaned again as he gathered his wits. He drove off, one hand on the wheel, the other not letting go of my hand. I should have reprimanded him—safety and all that—but the car was an automatic. Besides which, just feeling his soft warm skin was immensely soothing. His thumb gently rubbed the back of my hand and I simply focussed on how good that felt.

#22 Julius – Beta Earth

The front door banged open and Neith limped in, her arm around Paul's shoulder, who was all but carrying her along. All of Ramin's relaxed warmth evaporated and he quickly told Julius to move as Paul helped Neith onto the sofa. She groaned as Clio burst into the room and knelt in front of her.

'Bollocks, Paul. Why didn't you have her back? Here, have some salts. Ramin, quick,' she said and snapped her fingers, and Ramin dropped a variety of pills into Clio's hand. Julius stood back and watched as Neith's teammates dashed in and out to get water, and Ramin rubbed some gel on the back of her head. The three were arguing with each other, taking it in turns to blame each other, when Neith's voice cut across them.

'Enough. I'll live. Survived worse. A sucker punch to the back of the head is a coward's weapon, although it felt like a steel bar.'

'No, it was definitely a punch,' said Ramin. 'Julius saw it happen and said we needed to go back and get you.'

Neith laughed weakly. 'My hero. Cheers!'

'You saw what happened?' Paul asked cautiously.

Julius stared at the man who had punched Neith in the back of the head. He may be absent-minded, easily distracted, unaware of the bigger picture, but no one had ever accused Julius of being stupid.

'Yeah, it was so quick, some chap hit your friend there and she fell down.'

'Did you see who it was?'

'Christ, no, it all happened so fast. Do you want me to try to do like a photofit or an ID sketch?'

Paul watched him closely and then continued. 'No need, I saw him,' he said, then turned to Neith. 'Do we need to debrief now, or would you like a bath first? Warm up a bit?'

She smiled. 'A bath sounds a fine idea, but we won't all fit, not with Julius here. By the way,' she said, turning to Julius, 'do you have a middle name or a nickname we could use instead of Julius?'

Sensing his puzzlement, she shook her head, wincing as she did. 'Ignore me. Okay, so I... Sorry, hang on. Bucket...'

Clio suddenly whipped a bucket from the side of the sofa and Neith threw up into it. She took a sip of water and then apologised to Julius again.

'Blows to the head always make me vomit, as do all the pills to make me better. However, better out than in. Right, let's get on with it.'

Neith appeared to visibly revive and the team began to relax as they re-grouped around the table. Julius tried to sit as far away from any of them, and as close to the front door, as was possible.

'First things first,' began Neith, addressing Julius. 'You can leave anytime you want. The front door is unlocked, and no one here will stop you. However, before you do that, can I lay my cards on the table and offer my genuine, *our* genuine regrets, for the death of your friend Charles?'

Julius looked at the four faces and accepted their condolences. For now, despite his serious concerns, they appeared to offer no immediate threat.

'So, who are you? And why are those men after me?'

Neith took a sip of hot chocolate. 'Do you know, I think this fixes more ills than all your health kits combined?' She paused, then looked at Julius as she gathered her thoughts.

'You've clearly worked out we're not police.'

'Neith!'

'Quiet. He's not an idiot and we need his trust. We won't get it by lying to him.'

Clio continued to glare at Julius.

'We aren't police. We're a private security unit employed by an individual. He values his wealth as much as his privacy, and he heard that a Fabergé item was being talked about on the black web.'

Julius knew bugger all about the black web, but he was going to nod along until something made sense.

'We don't think the gossip came from your friend. He appears to have been a remarkably discreet individual. We think the rumour mill started with the dealer your friend met in London. Our boss dispatched us to intercede on his behalf and make a private bid. He didn't wish it to come to the surface. As you know, that meeting was interrupted by an unknown party. We don't know who they are, but we're quite confident that they don't have the egg yet and for some reason, presumably your closeness to Charles, they believe you are the clue to its discovery.'

Julius looked at them, alarmed. 'I don't have a clue where the egg is, but I do think I know a bit about it, if that helps?'

Four bodies leaned forward.

'I think it's an unknown egg.'

Neith looked surprised. 'Have you seen it?'

'No, deduction only I'm afraid.'

'Talk me through it.'

And so, Julius went on to discuss the size and age of the doll case, and the attached family history. Finally, he concluded that unless the paperwork had been tampered with in 1922, this had to be an unknown egg. Every other imperial egg had been sighted after 1918.

'Although, of course, it could be a non-imperial egg but I think if you consider that the grandfather was stationed at Yekaterinburg, then that makes the most sense.' He trailed off, uncomfortable with the team's scrutiny.

'Told you he was good,' Neith said with satisfaction.

'So, what now? I've told the police everything I know. I've told you everything I know. And it turns out what I know is almost nothing. I just want this done, and to get back to my normal life.'

There was a pause, then Ramin coughed. 'That's exactly what we want as well. We're going to be monitoring you for the next few days,' he said in a rush as Julius got ready to protest. 'We'll be totally unobtrusive. You won't even know we're there, but if you need us, just shout. I believe you have Neith's number in your phone contacts. You can also call if you want to discuss anything you remember, no matter how trivial. We aim to have this resolved in the next three days. And then you can forget you ever met us. Now, let me drive you home. I imagine you've had enough of us. Unless you'd rather stay?'

Julius stood up so fast that he had to pick up his chair, and he was standing by the door before Ramin had finished his question.

#23 Julius – Beta Earth

It was only a short drive out to Milton, but even so, Julius was glad it was Ramin driving and not Paul.

'She's a bit cavalier, isn't she?'

Ramin tried to reply, thinking through the meaning of the unfamiliar term.

'You know, always running ahead, not asking for opinions, doing things without asking,' said Julius.

'Aha, yes. *In the tree.*'

Now it was Julius' turn to pause, confused.

'Monkey in the Tree. A Monkey. One that runs ahead, pays no attention to others. Dances to their own drum.'

'Oh, yes. That describes her. Are you lot French then? I still don't have much of a handle on you guys.'

Ramin laughed. 'The less you know, the safer you are. Anyway, *cavalier* isn't quite the right term. In the tree is a compliment. It means she's a leader, a fighter. She sees ahead and plans alternatives in a gunshot. She's like a major or general on a battlefield. She leads from the front, inspiring and protecting.'

'You need to brush up on modern political warfare. Since when do leaders lead from the front?'

'Fair enough. Maybe like a knight or king, from days gone by?'

'Oh God, how mortifying,' said Julius. 'I've been rescued by a knight like some damsel in distress.'

Ramin laughed. 'You'd look good in a dress; you've got the legs for it.'

'Distress. A damsel in distress. Not a dress. But thank you.'

'You're welcome.'

As they drove on, Julius began to relax in Ramin's company. He wasn't sure what to make of the strange team. Every time he thought he had an idea of who they were, they did something to confound him. He was still reeling from the death of Charlie, but he had to trust someone.

'Can I ask a question?' he asked.

Ramin smiled whilst swerving to avoid a cyclist. 'Damn, why do they fill the road full of moving targets. Sorry, carry on.'

'How well do you all know each other? You four, I mean?' Julius wasn't sure if he should say anything or if he was making his position even more vulnerable. So far though, this team appeared to have saved his skin rather than flayed it. But still, there was something wrong with them in a way that he just couldn't put his finger on.

'Forever! Well, Neith and I have literally known each other since childhood. She and Clio became firm friends in the first year of training and Paul joined our unit as my partner two years back. He and Neith have an on-again, off-again relationship, and we have worked as a team of four a few times. You're safe with us.'

Avoiding another cyclist, he looked over at an unconvinced Julius. 'Is there a problem?'

The last few days had been a paranoid nightmare for Julius. He liked the strange girl that summoned nightmares and flicked him goofy thumbs up, in a church of all places. He didn't like the fact that no one had her back, and so he decided to trust Ramin.

'In the churchyard, when you and that mad woman drove me away, I was watching the fight from the back window of the car. Neith was watching the car when she was punched in the back of the head.'

'Hmm.' Ramin nodded, scowling. 'You told us this already?'

'The thing is, I did see who hit her. It was your team member. Paul.'

There was silence, then Ramin looked across at Julius. 'No, I think you must be mistaken. He's too good a fighter.'

'It wasn't an accident.'

'Okay. Then you must have got the men muddled up. We were all wearing black. There is absolutely no way he would deliberately attack her.'

Julius fell silent. He knew what he'd seen, but he wasn't going to press the point. Ramin was adamant, and Julius didn't want to make his own situation any worse.

As they pulled up at the house, Ramin got out first and asked Julius for the house keys, telling Julius to wait in the car. He let himself in, and a few moments later returned and waved for Julius to join him. Julius watched as Ramin attached a few tiny cameras to his front and back door, and then two more in the front and rear bedrooms, looking over the street and the back alley. He then downloaded an app on Julius' phone and showed him how to monitor the cameras.

'Call us if you need anything,' he said, 'and honestly, Paul is one of the good guys. That was a pretty intense scene back there. Easy to get confused.'

Julius nodded and watched as Ramin drove away. One thing he knew for sure was that Paul had sucker-punched Neith, and the minute he did, the other men had stopped fighting.

#24 Neith – Beta Earth

No matter how many pills and potions, hot baths and hot toddies you take, a blow to the back of the head stays with you. I was completely fed up. There was no way I should have allowed a Beta operative to get the drop on me like that. Only their truly elite fighters were a match for us, and this lot were acting like local wallies. I was cross and grumpy, and too much was going wrong in ways I hadn't foreseen. I needed to shake off this sense of impending doom.

'Clio, grab your coat, we're going to the pub. Ramin, keep a watch on Julius' tracker and keep monitoring all the local airways.'

When Ramin had administered the analgesic to Julius' bruises, he had slipped in a subdermal tracker. It would monitor the man's heart rate, chemical additives, adrenaline levels and location; basic stuff that would alert us if anything started to go wrong. It also had a mic so we could monitor all his conversations. The AI tracker would monitor all the usual stuff, and only alert us if it heard anything worth paying attention to. They were also designed to be easily dissolved after a few weeks in the body and easily deactivated via the use of a localised electromagnetic pulse. There had been a lot of ethics committees on the use of these, but despite all these safeguards they were declared illegal without written consent. They were also going to be outlawed for use on Beta Earth, but the powers that be made an effective argument for the citizens of Beta Earth being of diminished responsibility. Therefore, they are one of the groups legally authorised to be fitted with trackers without their prior consent. Children, criminals, mentally incapacitated and Betas. So far no one had complained. Plus, it's hard to complain if you don't know about it.

There was a large pub at the end of the road, and it seemed a fairly popular venue as we pushed our way through the crowd to find a table towards a quiet corner at the back of the pub. I settled down and waited for Clio to come back with our drinks.

'How are you, boss? I made them put a cherry in it.'

Clio didn't always master the local customs, and I found myself looking at a pint of stout with half a cherry balancing on top of the foam.

'He asked if this was some new hipster trend. I said it was. Did I get it wrong?'

'A cherry on top is one of those sayings, although you do get them on cupcakes, knickerbocker glories, and I think Babychams. It's not usually associated with pints, but maybe you'll have started a trend. No harm, no foul. Not like when you ended up convincing half of mediaeval England that a scented pomander could keep the plague away.'

'That was a joke. How could I know they were going to take it seriously?'

'People get a bit desperate when facing mass death. You need to remember a bit of subtlety. Speaking of which, you kicked Julius a bit hard?'

Clio scowled. This was as close as the two of us came to reprimands and neither of us liked it particularly. I was by far the better fighter, but she was no slouch. If anything she was too enthusiastic, preferring to finish a conflict to the point of long-term incapacitation. I much preferred that my assailant simply got out of my way. She preferred that they were so far out of the way as to be in another continent or coffin. Her kill count was about the same as mine. Her figure bothered her less than mine did. I know that deep down she considered herself the better fighter for this exact reason. By Beta standards, she'd be right.

'He wasn't permanently injured.'

'No, but he was injured to the extent that he was hard to manoeuvre off the field of play. A little more finesse next time.' I smiled, taking the sting out of my words, and ate the cherry, which was surprisingly nice with the stout. Maybe she'd started something new after all.

'Clee, I think we've got a serious problem. I think there's a second Alpha team operating here and I don't think they're on our side.'

I watched as Clio took a sip of her drink, never once breaking her eye contact with me. She put her glass back on the table and let out a big sigh.

'I agree. It's the only explanation that makes any sense, other than we've got a rogue member within the team, and that's a non-starter.'

I nodded. Like her, I had considered it, though I then discounted the idea.

'So how do you want to proceed?'

'I'm going to instigate Level Three precautions.' Not total overkill, but enough to keep us alert.

'Not Level Four?'

I shook my head. Level Four would include stepping a team member back to Alpha. The last time that had happened had been twenty years ago when the team had accidentally got caught up in a civil war and a roadside bomb. Not everyone had made it back, and the team leader had been publicly censured for not preventing the loss of life. I didn't feel the situation here was that precarious, but something was wrong. And if I was honest, it wasn't just on this side that I thought things were going wrong.

'Is there something else you're worried about?' Clio asked. 'You've got that look?'

I'm pretty certain I didn't have a "look". We work hard on not having "looks". That said, Clio was at the top of her game and we had known each other for years. I remembered the first time we had met. She had been so bristly, ready to fight anyone that looked at her funny. She thought I had, so we ended up fighting to a standstill, both of us with bleeding noses, broken fingers and black eyes. We'd been put on a week's hard labour and become instant best friends. If I truly had a "look" she'd be the one to spot it. The only person that knew me better was Ramin.

'I'm going to get Ramin to send the angel tomorrow as well. Let Sam know of our problems.'

Clio narrowed her eyes. Deploying an angel was a serious step. The problem with the Q Field was that it was almost too sophisticated to use. We couldn't just send stuff through it like messages or artefacts; they left, but they never arrived. We still don't know what happens to them. Maybe there's a universe somewhere that keeps receiving stuff, although mostly we've stopped now. It was getting tiresome.

But we still needed to be able to communicate with Alpha Earth, even if it was only one-way. Generally, one of the first things a team would do would be to identify an *angel*. This was usually an old person with a terminal illness and no relatives. We would approach them, and explain the benefits, a full cure, and the drawbacks, this was a one-way ticket. Once we had convinced them we weren't talking about heaven—and you'd be amazed how often we had to rule that out—most were up for it. Once on Alpha, they would hand over the message and then be taken off for treatment. They would then spend the rest of their time giving lectures to students about Beta ways, as well as travelling or just enjoying their new extended life. The vast majority adjusted perfectly. A couple felt that heaven should look less like upper Egypt. So, we shipped them off to New Zealand. That seemed to work.

But like I said, their deployment was rare.

'Do you want me to do this?' asked Clio, 'or is this one of those touchy-feely things?'

'Touchy-feely things. This is more Ramin's bag.'

'I've never actually killed an angel you know!'

'I know,' I said, and laughed, then got up from the table. 'My round.'

This was a good call. I could feel my concerns not exactly disappearing, but getting back into perspective. Maybe it was the company, or maybe it was the cherry. Either way, it was working. I laughed, thinking of Clio trying to convince an angel to leave this mortal coil.

I sat back down and handed Clio her drink. 'Angels aside, I think there's more going on. The thing is, I've been noticing problems at home. Like, since when do we rescue totemic artefacts? And what's with Ramin and Paul not finding their missing treasure?'

Clio took a drink. 'Honestly, honey, I think you're jumping at shadows. I'll grant you that something is wrong on this side but if you start running after loose threads you may compromise this mission?'

I stared up at the ceiling and exhaled. The problem with being the leader was trying to anticipate every problem, which was bound to make you look down rabbit holes. The trick was not to go down them.

'You think I'm overreacting?'

'No,' Clio said, quick to jump in. 'Curses no, you are usually right on the money. It's just if there is something going on back home, I doubt it has anything to do with this mission. And if there was something going on back home, more serious brains than ours will already be monitoring it. But, I tell you what, when we get home, I'll start doing a bit of quiet research.'

And that's why we have teams. One person can never see both sides of a coin at the same time. We drank our pints, and that was the last time we laughed together.

Interlude 2

The following text conversation was retrieved, doing a sweep of the ghost files of the Q Zone security system. It has been added to the evidence report for Case No: 234530/H. As yet neither correspondent has been identified.

- Just to let you know we have intercepted an angel from the live team. It looks like they are having problems and are aware that someone may be after the egg; they suspect foul play.
- Why are you contacting me to tell me you are screwing up?
- I just thought you would like to be kept in the loop.
- Do you think for a minute you could report in a straightforward manner? Need I remind you that we want the egg. If you fail to deliver it, the repercussions for you will be severe.

- Are you threatening me? It works both ways, you know.

- No, it doesn't. Your disgrace will be front-page news whereas we will simply slip beneath the typeface.

- There's no need for—

- You contacted us. Don't get in touch again until you are able to arrange the handover of the egg.

#25 Neith – Beta Earth

The following morning I woke refreshed; cherries in stout and good company had soothed out the blow to the back of my head and I felt human again. We had two days until the retrieval point, and I was beginning to buzz. As you get closer to a fixed point, you can't help but react. I know some teams that approach it in a nearly Zen-like state. However, with the cock-ups and unseen opponents playing interference, I was not channelling the Zen-like part of my psyche. To be fair, I wasn't even certain if I had a Zen-like part to my psyche. What I did have was a countdown.

'Ramin, I need you to send the angel.'

The team looked up at me. Sending an angel meant we were in trouble.

'Are you sure?' asked Paul.

'I'm instigating Level Three. I want us all to run a sweep on ourselves for trackers. I want fifteen-minute, simple buzz check-ins and hourly reports. I want full personal surveillance until the mission is completed.'

Clio picked at her teeth. These were Level Four procedures in all but name.

'Boss, do you not think—'

I cut her off. I had taken her advice from the night before and she was probably right, maybe there was nothing untoward going on back home, and even if there was, it wasn't going to be connected to us. But here? Here, there was definitely untoward stuff going on.

'Since we arrived, the old woman in Poland was found dead. Charles and the dealer were gunned down in broad daylight. By a car that Paul didn't notice. Let that sink in for a minute.' I paused. Paul was one of Alpha's finest surveillance guys. 'Furthermore, the car was abandoned, and the occupants managed to evade *all* the cameras in the vicinity and leave no trace of having tampered with the surveillance network. Two men broke into Charles' house and referred to a woman who was giving instructions. These may have been the same men in the drive-by shooting, but they weren't the same men at the memorial service.' I took a breath. 'Now, the memorial service. This team not only knew to target Julius, but they also knew about us as they split in two, leaving a team outside. How did we miss that? Clio, you were the last one in? How did you miss a second team?'

I hated questioning the others like this. I was all but accusing them of incompetence, but for someone to have evaded notice they had to be specially trained.

'I've told you already, when I came into the building the perimeter was clear. Paul had run a sweep and there were no anomalous cars or pedestrians in the vicinity.'

Paul scowled, as well he might. That was twice now that he had been the one who failed to spot a problem. At the very least, when we got home I was going to have to recommend him for a refresher course in surveillance. Which was going to be insulting.

'I'm telling you, Clio, the coast was clear. I honestly think we have a second team out there.'

'Right,' she scoffed, 'or the more likely scenario is that you screwed up.'

Paul looked sick, and I was worried that morale was plummeting.

'Enough. Let's not forget that this second team was good enough to get the drop on me at the church.'

'Maybe you were too busy smiling at the shit fly?' said Clio, her tone dangerously pointed. The boys went quiet. This was not a good time to fall out.

'Clio, can you for once not refer to Betas as *shit flies*? His name is Julius. He is an asset, a civilian, and innocent. It is our duty to protect him, and I am quite capable of doing two things at once. Whoever this team is, they are pretty much our match, and I don't like it.' My voice was rising, and I turned so that I was now addressing all three of them. 'So, do you think instead of blaming each other we can get it together and stop fucking up?'

Ramin leant across the kitchen table and squeezed my hand. 'Sorry, boss. What else do you need us to do?'

I took a deep breath. 'First principles. I want you to go over each other's work. See if you can spot anything out of place. This is not a rebuke, but when you first looked you were not looking with the knowledge that someone may be running interference. This is simply a fresh pair of eyes. And yes, I'm including my work in this. We'll keep it within the teams, so Clio, you can evaluate my research and decisions, and vice versa. The same for you two,' I said, looking at Paul and Ramin. 'In addition, Ramin, I need you to set up the angel and I'll give you the message to send with them. I think we have to assume that the second team will also be at the egg's final extraction point, and I don't want to get caught out a third time. Let's try to grab the egg before then and get the hell home. Be vigilant!'

I gave Ramin our mission notes and hoped that when Sam received them, he agreed with my assessment. Mission notes delivered via an angel weren't a call for help. No help was coming, but if we failed to return, the people back home would have some clues. Call it our Black Box flight recorder. Clio and Paul sat down in front of their laptops and started running through the data, whilst keeping an eye on Julius' tracker. If he so much as hiccupped, we would know all about it.

I looked up as Ramin closed the front door behind him. I was having to stop myself from sending Clio or Paul with him, but I knew that was a waste of resources. Not to mention insulting to Ramin's skills. It's just that I had never felt so jumpy on a mission before. When you lead a team into the field, you feel bad if you fail to achieve your objective. I don't know how you'd feel if you failed to retrieve your team. It wasn't a thought I was happy with, but it had been slowly building over the past few days. Being responsible for them, though, didn't mean the same thing as getting in their way. I just had to trust in them to get us all out of here. Egg or no egg, it was the first time I had ever thought of abandoning a mission.

Shaking myself, I pulled on my running shoes. I needed exercise. I wasn't up to sparring yet, but I felt edgy stuck in the house. Some fresh air and endorphins would get my brain firing and help me see this mission with a bit more clarity. As I got to the driveway, I heard the front door close behind me and saw Paul looking concerned.

'About the angel. I was thinking. I think you should send me over instead. Let me catch up with Ramin, and I'll go instead of the angel.'

I looked at him, amazed.

'It's not that bad! An angel will do fine. And I need all of you here.'

This was so defeatist. I didn't know what to say. I knew he was unhappy because of the mistakes he had been making, but running away wasn't going to fix it. This wasn't like Paul.

'I just think you'll have more chance of success if I go over and warn Sam directly of what's happening.'

'I said no, Paul.'

'But—'

'No!' What was wrong with him? Snapping, I told him to get back indoors and carry on with the tasks that did need to be done.

'We need you here. Just follow your orders and everything will be fine.'

As last words, I could have done better.

#26 Sam – Alpha Earth

'Sir, something bloody odd's just happened.'

Sam Nymens looked up. It had been a quiet week. "Bloody odd" should be interesting.

'The Q Field just shut down. The portal map flashed red at every location and then reset itself as though nothing had happened.'

'What?'

'The Q Field shut down.'

'That's not bloody odd,' he roared, and ran along the corridors to the Q Field area. As he entered the room, it was full of technicians, each person typing madly on keyboards, pulling holo screens up and swearing loudly. Sam yelled for quiet and demanded a report. Farnaz Beckett was station head for the second shift, and as one of the three shift heads, everything that happened during the shift was her responsibility. She came over as her staff ran up to her with fresh read-outs. Giving quick instructions, she sent them back to their stations. Sam was glad to see it was her shift. She was a stickler for details and her shift team were terrifyingly prompt in filing end of shift reports. They were nicknamed the Dull Shift, and that's the way they liked it.

Now looking around the room, it was anything but dull. As she stood in front of Sam, he saw that she was torn between wanting to give a full report whilst also wanting to get back to the problem at hand.

'Sir, the gate pulsed and went dead ten minutes ago. There was a delay of sixty-five seconds and then it just switched back on. So far, none of the read-outs report that anything happened. If we hadn't seen it with our own eyes, we wouldn't have known that anything had happened.'

'How is that possible?'

'Sir, I have no idea. I'm running diagnostics on the hardware and the software, and I'm going to have all personnel screened in case of a mass hallucinogenic incident.'

Sam paused. The people in this room were the best in their field. It hadn't even occurred to him to test the staff.

'How many teams do we have on Beta right now?' This was the first concern. Without knowing if the system was safe, he didn't want them stepping back through. Nor did he want to send anyone to warn them.

'Four teams right now. Diana and Johannes are due today, Piers and Qiang are due next week. We have a live event ending tomorrow, and there are four in that team.'

Sam didn't need the technician to name them, as he always knew who was on a live event.

'Is the Step safe? Can we find out before Di and Jo return?'

'Ma'am, sir!' a technician shouted out. 'The portal map!' All eyes turned to the screen, where masses of thin yellow lines were fracturing out from multiple radial points.

'Yellow?! But that's temporal anomalies.'

'Record this. Use a physical camera! Don't trust the system.'

Everyone grabbed phones and eyepieces, and some went as far as to grab pen and paper. No one had ever said "Don't Trust the System" before. As they watched and sketched, the yellow lines began to fracture further and faster until it looked as if the entire screen was a solid wall of yellow. Then in a flash of light, all the yellow lines disappeared, and the map returned to normal.

'What the fuck! Farnaz?'

Farnaz was shouting to engineers and typing madly on a keyboard whilst looking at a holo display in front of her.

'That did not just happen.'

'What?'

'What we saw, the system has no trace of it and is also reporting no anomalies, neither spatial nor temporal. According to the system, nothing just happened.' She took a deep breath. 'Sam, I cannot vouch for the safety of the Q Step. I recommend that no one from this side steps through until we've done a full evaluation.'

'Cat's teeth, Farnaz, what about those on the other side?'

'Sir, all we can do is wait.'

'Can we close it?'

'Sir?'

'Can we close it and stop them from stepping through?'

'Potentially yes, but what if we can't open it up again? Or what if closing it breaks the current link?'

'And what if them stepping through splices them into a thousand quantum states?'

'Sam, it's not my call. If we close it, I think we almost certainly will lose them. If we leave it open, I don't know. Had I just walked in here I would say that the system is working perfectly.'

Sam glared. 'Right. I'm going to see the chancellor. Tell me if anything else happens, and I want fifteen-minute updates.'

The chancellor was enjoying a glass of port. This morning's tasks had been successful, and he felt he deserved a reward. The living was easy, and life was good.

'We have a problem,' announced Samuel Nymens as he burst into the office, no knocking, no deference due to the chancellor's rank, not even a decent salutation.

Nymens was one of those troublemakers who just never knew when to do as he was told. Heading up the Step division made him act as though he was pharaoh. He wasn't even Egyptian, and there were rumours he wasn't even a fully qualified archivist, having come through the German School of Curators who were known to have a lax system of nomenclature.

'Is it so serious that you have forgotten how to knock? A simple act that separates the uncivilised man from the mannered gentleman. Was it not Selassie that said—'

'The Q Step is broken,'

Soliman choked on his drink. 'What do you mean? It can't be broken; I was down there myself not an hour ago and everything was fine.'

'Well, it's not now. And why were you down there? I wasn't informed?'

'This is my mouseion, Nymens, I can go where I want. Now I repeat, what do you mean, broken? Is it a simple misalignment of the vortices or the stars?'

Sam interrupted him. Soliman knew bugger all about quantum mechanics and could often be heard waxing lyrical about its poetic qualities. It was enough to make a grown man drink port.

'I mean broken, as in flashing lights then no lights then weird noises then silence.'

'My God. Has anyone been injured? Has flesh been torn asunder from the frail bones of a naïve operative?'

'No one has been hurt. You're not going to be fired or sued. Yet. We still have three teams totalling eight people out in the field. We don't know whether to send a volunteer or wait to see if they step back safely.'

'I thought you said it was broken.'

'It was. Now it seems to be fine.'

'Great Ra, man, which is it? Is it broken or working?'

'That's just it, we don't know until we test it with a live subject. Which will be me by the way. I just thought we should let you know what was happening.'

'For God's sake man you're blathering like an idiot. Let me see what's happening.' Pushing his body up from the table, he swaggered to the door. In his youth he had been noted for his poetics and athletics, now his muscles were turning softer than the slush he called his sonic soliloquies. Once a month people would gather to listen to him perform at the local open mic night. Sam took note of all who attended and made sure they were never appointed to positions requiring taste, judgement or rationality.

Interlude 3

The following text conversation was retrieved, doing a sweep of the ghost files of the Q Zone security system. It has been added to the evidence report for Case No: 234530/H. As yet neither correspondent has been identified.

- What the bollocky fuck was that?

- That wasn't us. We assumed you had somehow screwed up.

- What? Are you insane? Do you think we would tamper with the golden goose?

- So, it wasn't you either. This is alarming. I await your update and I will report to the others that this isn't your screw up that you are aware of.

- This isn't our scre—

Conversation terminated.

- Bollocks.

27 Julius – Beta Earth

The sound of footsteps disturbed Julius and he looked up from the screen where he was cataloguing new acquisitions. An archivist walked past, offering a warm smile as they went about their business. Julius felt the disappointment and loneliness. Those were not Charlie's footsteps. He would never be interrupted or annoyed by his footsteps again. Yesterday they'd held his memorial service, and he had become involved in a fight and then practically kidnapped by a group of four suspicious individuals. He was pretty certain they weren't involved in Charlie's death, but they were all over the retrieval of the Fabergé egg. He wished he could help them and get them out of his life. He'd had enough "excitement" to last a lifetime.

He checked his phone. He was due to have lunch with Rebecca in half an hour and he was determined not to be late; the distraction would be welcome. Plus, he didn't want to let her down again. He could tell she was fed up and ready to give him the old heave-ho. He couldn't blame her, and if he were honest, his heart wasn't in the relationship anyway. They had nothing in common, but as long as she seemed to want to date him he had gone along with it. Now he felt their time was coming to an end.

So much was changing. It had only been a couple of weeks ago when Charlie had burst in here full of excitement on the brink of a historic discovery. And where were they now? Charlie was dead, Julius was being pursued by strangers and the egg was nowhere to be found. What had Charlie done with it? Was it here in Cambridge? A Fabergé egg hiding in some dusty corner, lost for another hundred years? Maybe it was tucked away somewhere, and a fastidious cleaner would knock it out of its cubby hole. Julius smiled at the image. Would that make it theirs? Was it finders, keepers?

In his will, Charlie had left his house and worldly goods to Julius, with a silly note saying that he'd never be able to afford his own place if he insisted on never leaving the stacks. Charlie's parents had smiled and agreed it was a good decision. They didn't need the money, but they did come and collect a few of his possessions to take back to the US. As Julius hugged them, he thought that they would never live in the UK again. Maybe the egg was in the house? He was fairly confident it wasn't. The police had searched it, as had Neith, and whilst he was uncertain about the police's search skills he was under no illusions as to Neith's skill sets. So where was it?

Another set of footsteps stopped at his desk, and he saw one of the clerks standing quietly and waiting for Julius to notice him. A parcel had arrived at the main desk for him. Julius' heart quickened. Was it possible? Thanking the clerk, he moved quickly through the vaults, running up the last flight of steps and bursting through the doors to the front reception.

'There's a parcel for me?'

The staff at the desk first glared, then modified their expressions. They had been ready to scold a noisy undergraduate, but here stood Julius Strathclyde, one of their favourite and usually respectful professors, panting heavily and all but dancing on the spot.

Jane went to the pigeonhole to collect his parcel and returned with a clipboard for him to sign. Julius was easily her favourite researcher, and she had no idea why he was dating that dreadful girl with the perfect make-up and excessive opinions. She knew Julius wasn't into appearances. Many's the time she had to point out his jumper was back to front or inside out. Now, as she handed him the heavy box, he gave her a huge smile and she couldn't help but grin back. How lovely to have a man so excited by his research.

As Julius headed back to his desk, his excitement began to slip. This parcel was book-shaped and book heavy. He had a terrible feeling it was a book. Not the egg. As he unwrapped it, he saw it was from the University of Harvard and was a dictionary of one of the early native languages that he had asked to look at a few months ago. He had seen it online and thought he recognised the penmanship. It was a doodle in the margin that had caught his eye. However, whoever and whatever it was, it wasn't a priceless Fabergé egg, and it wasn't a clue from Charlie.

He flicked through the pages and realised he was right. This appeared to be written in the same hand as the one he had been tracking down through some English letters. A month ago, this would have been a stupendous revelation, but now his heart wasn't in it. The infamous disappearance of William Hare, notorious body snatcher, had finally been solved. He had fled to the New World and had refashioned himself as a learned gentleman. Now Julius just sighed and closed the volume.

Gathering up his work, he placed it in his cubicle then headed back to the main desk to ask them to keep the Harvard dictionary in their secure vault. He may as well go and meet Rebecca, see if she could cheer him up. He had just got to the front door when Jane called him back.

'Julius. I forgot, there's a postcard for you as well. I didn't see it in the pigeonhole.'

She waved a garish postcard with a local pub on the front, festooned in hanging baskets. Julius smiled, remembering the many times that he and Charlie had tumbled out of that pub at closing time. Taking the card, he wondered who on earth in Cambridge would be sending him a postcard. Turning it over, his heart stuttered as he saw Charlie's confident scrawl across the rear.

Franklin's hungry. Look up Lucky

What the hell did that mean? Julius gave Jane a quick hug, tucked the postcard into his jacket's inner breast pocket and headed back to the exit, feeling happier than he had in days. He wondered what Neith and her team would do if they knew about the card. She had said they were monitoring him, but it wasn't like they could track his heart rate or anything. He laughed, thinking about how they would have reacted in the past fifteen minutes when first he thought the book was the egg, and then he discovered an actual clue from Charlie.

Stepping out onto the street, the low wintry sunlight blinded him for a minute. He decided to take the back streets rather than try to navigate the bikes and tourists with the sun in his eyes. Checking his phone, he saw it was one pm. For once he wasn't going to be late meeting Rebecca, although he suspected he would be a poor conversationalist. Who was Franklin, and why were they hungry?

According to the postmark, Charlie had posted the card on the day he died, here in Cambridge. So, either the night before he left for London, or that morning, Charlie had posted Julius a postcard with an obscure message on it. Why? Julius could only think of one logical explanation. Charlie had hidden the egg and left Julius a clue as to its location. Deep in thought, Julius popped out of one of the lanes, once more into the blinding sunlight, and was startled by a strong hand grabbing his arm.

#28 Neith – Beta Earth

I had just been recalibrating the gun's harmonics when my wrist brace buzzed. Julius' tracker had just identified an anomaly. I flicked up the hologram and called Clio and Ramin into the room. Paul was in the town following another lead. Everyone's wrist brace would have pinged, so at least he knew to be ready in case we called him. We gathered around the laptop, where I had already pulled up the more in-depth readings from Julius' implant.

'What just happened?' asked Ramin.

'Massive spike in heart rate but seemed to calm down very quickly.'

'Where is he?'

'In the library vaults, he's been there all morning. He went to collect something which made his heart race, but then nothing.'

Clio pointed at the location section of the screen. 'Okay, he's stationary again. I'd say he's sitting down now. Alpha waves are engaged, cortisol levels are low. Looks like something intrigued him for a bit, but now he's sad again.'

'False alarm then. Come on, this is as good a time as any to take a break.' We headed to the kitchen and began to throw things together for a quick lunch. 'Clio, where are you on cross-checking my research? Anything I missed?'

Clio laughed. 'You seem to have failed for the umpteenth time to recommend me for awesome partner of the year award. But other than that, it all looks pretty acceptable. Although your filing remains slapdash.'

I grinned, grateful for her levity. 'Ramin? Anything in Paul's work?'

Ramin looked concerned. 'There're a few things, but I'm not sure yet. I think I want to run them past him first.'

'Don't be an idiot,' said Clio. 'If he's screwed up we need to know about it, and now. Not after he's had a chance to cover it up.'

'Enough, Clio. If Paul has screwed up, he'll own it. He won't try to weasel out. Ramin, what have you found? Clio is right. It can't wait. If Paul has made a mistake he can explain later, but if it means we have an active breach we have—'

All three wrist braces chimed, and I broke off what I was saying and flicked up the hologram again.

'Bloody hell!'

'Look at that heartbeat. Adrenaline is spiking. Alpha waves erratic.'

'Where is he?'

'Main reception. Now leaving the building.'

I called Paul. He had also seen the spike and I told him to go and get eyes on Julius but to hang back until I joined him. I returned my attention to the other two.

'Do you think he has the egg?' asked Clio.

'Possibly. Ramin, stay in the house, full obs on all personnel. Clio, with me, but hang back as far as you can whilst retaining visuals. I'm going to "bump" into Julius and find out what's happening.'

Grabbing my coat, I ran out of the house and casually began jogging into town. Ramin was in my earpiece giving me a running update.

'I think you need to speed up, Julius' route is erratic.'

'What?'

'He keeps nipping down little lanes. It looks like basic counter-surveillance moves.'

'Is he running?'

'No. But, nope… He's just turned again. He is definitely not taking an obvious route to anywhere.'

'Okay. I'm going to be there in five minutes.'

If he thought he was being followed, then he probably was. I sped up from a jog to a run, dumping my long puffer coat as I raced towards Julius.

'He's now emerging from a lane onto a main thoroughfare and… Hell!'

'What? Ramin, what's happened?' I sprinted towards town.

'The signal's gone dead!'

'Paul!' There was no response. 'Ramin, tell Paul to get to the last known location.'

'Neith, Paul's signal has also gone dead. I've lost both their signals!'

That wasn't possible. That had to be a conscious decision. Paul's tracker was nothing like the ones we put on Beta subjects. Our trackers were integral parts of our kit and couldn't be easily overrun by a sweeper. Even death didn't switch them off. Only a manual override did that.

'Neith. Treat Paul as hostile,' said Ramin.

What was Ramin saying? In what universe would I not trust Paul?

'Ramin, are you kidding? Clio? Can you hear this?'

'Neith. I'm only talking to you. This is a direct line. Something is wrong, and right now you are the only person I have any faith in.'

#29 Julius – Beta Earth

'Hello again.'

Julius pulled back in annoyance and was alarmed as the hand tightened its grip. The sun was blinding him, and he still couldn't see his assailant, but the voice sounded familiar. The man stepped in front of the sun.

'There, now can you see me?'

With alarm, Julius recognised the man from Neith's team, the one that had felled her with a punch to the head. The one that the rest of the team trusted.

'What do you want? Get your hand off me.'

'I will, but just to let you know, if you run or shout out, I will kill Rebecca.'

Julius froze as the other man smiled at him.

'Excellent,' he said, and smiled as he released Julius' arm. 'Now, let's go and join her, shall we? You don't want to keep her waiting. You know how much she doesn't like that. She's sitting in Mulligan's right now. Come on.'

And with that he crossed the road and headed towards the café, leaving Julius with no option but to follow him. Maybe he could play along? But why had he threatened to kill Rebecca? Was he no longer pretending to be a good guy? As they got to the front door, Julius confronted him.

'I can't remember your name,' Julius hissed. 'Does Neith know you're here?'

'Of course she does. Neith is always in control. Did you fall for her "trust me I'm a good guy" routine?'

He laughed as Julius' face fell.

'Never mind. I'm Paul by the way. Now, let's go and say hello to Rebecca. Just follow my lead and no one will get hurt.'

The gentle hubbub of a lunchtime serving was in full swing, and the warmth of the kitchen enveloped them as they walked in. But Julius was shaking. All he wanted to do was divert this man and try to get Rebecca to safety.

'Hello, darling. You're almost on time. What a lovely surprise,' Rebecca said as she put her phone away and looked up, waiting for Julius to kiss her on the cheeks. She then put her hand out to Paul. 'Hello?'

'How do you do?' Paul leant forward and shook her hand, smiling as he did so. 'Paul Flint, a colleague of Julius' visiting from Prague. I hope you don't mind my joining you. I'm new in town and when I asked where was good to eat, he suggested I have lunch with you both. Mind you, I'm amazed Julius here was prepared to share your company.'

Laughing at Julius, he gave him a playful punch on the arm. 'You are a sly old dog. Fancy not mentioning how beautiful Rebecca is.'

Rebecca demurred prettily but pulled out the chair closest to her and invited him to sit down. As he did so, he turned and raised an eyebrow at Julius.

The waitress came to take their order. When Julius said he wasn't hungry, Paul laughed and ordered him a portion of chips.

'Can't have you fading away on poor Rebecca here. A girl like her needs a strong man by her side.'

Julius felt sick. Why was Rebecca simpering like an idiot? If she couldn't sense how dangerous he was, surely she should be revolted by his appalling chat up lines.

Paul and Rebecca made small talk about her job until the food arrived. She was oblivious to Julius' discomfort as she talked about her recent promotion and her dreams of working in London. As the waitress put down their food, Paul leant forward and dipped some chips into the sauce. The tables around them were busy with conversation and now that their food had been delivered, they wouldn't be interrupted again.

'So, let's get down to business. What caused your heartbeat to surge at twelve forty-five?'

Rebecca looked puzzled, as the topic and tone of the conversation seemed to have veered off course.

'Julius? Is something wrong with your heart?'

Paul turned back to her, the smile on his face now cold and flinty. 'Eat your lunch like a good girl. The men are talking.' As Rebecca recoiled, ready to retort, he swung his head back to Julius. 'Tell her.'

'Rebecca, please listen to me. This man is not a friend. I believe he's involved in the murder of Charlie.

You are perfectly safe, but please just stay quiet and calm.'

'That's right, darling. Quiet and calm, and you'll be perfectly safe. I have a gun in my hand under the table, pointing at your guts. One word from you and I'll blow you wide open.'

Rebecca made to stand up, but with his free hand, Paul grabbed her wrist and squeezed it hard.

'Quiet and calm.'

Terrified, Rebecca sat back down and took a shaky sip of soup after Paul instructed her to eat.

'Now then,' he said as he returned his attention to Julius, 'twelve forty-five. What happened?'

Julius studied the café. Neith had said she would be watching him, but no one seemed to be coming to the rescue. Maybe Paul was right, maybe Neith had also been stringing him along. But despite hardly knowing the woman, he trusted her. She wasn't in on this.

'I received an antique ledger from Harvard that I've been waiting on for a few months. It reveals something that is quite a breakthrough in my field.'

'Ah, so that's what that was,' said Paul. 'But I think you'll find that was at twelve thirty. What happened at twelve forty-five? And please don't lie.'

Julius considered prevaricating, but what was the point. Somehow this man had been tracking his heartbeat. God knows how, maybe he could even read his mind? Charlie was dead, and Rebecca was in danger through no fault of her own. Whatever else he could do; he could try to get her out of this.

'I received a postcard from Charlie.'

Rebecca looked up from her soup, her eyes wide. 'Oh, Julius!'

Frowning, Paul looked at Rebecca. 'Did I say you could talk?'

Looking back at Julius, he smiled with pleasure. 'Let's have it then.'

Julius considered lying, but the fear on Rebecca's face was unbearable. He might not love the girl, but he didn't want to play any part in her prolonged misery. He pulled out the postcard from his pocket and handed it over to Paul, who promptly turned it over.

'What the hell does that mean?'

'No idea. I think he meant it to be difficult to understand.'

'Look up? Where?'

'I think he was in a hurry. I think he wanted me to look up Benjamin Franklin, maybe. I don't know. I only just got the bloody card. Maybe there's something under the stamp?'

'If you think…' Paul was distracted by his watch and he studied it, swearing quietly. 'Well, this has been lovely, but the cavalry are on their way. Got to run. Sit still and don't try to follow me.'

#30 Neith – Beta Earth

I was running across the bridge now and almost at Julius' last known location. It was the same place where Paul's wrist brace had switched off its geo-tag. I carried on talking to Ramin.

'This is madness, but I'm going to play along. You can explain later, but I'm alerting Clio. She needs to know that Paul has gone off-grid.'

Opening up a direct channel to Clio, I told her what Ramin had just said, leaving off the bit that he wasn't currently trusting her either.

'I think Ramin's right. Why else would Paul have switched his comms off? And it would explain who's been running interference.'

It explained nothing as far as I was concerned. I liked Paul. A lot. He was my friend, and sometimes a very enthusiastic bedfellow. What he wasn't, was an enemy. Surely? And why? None of it made any sense. We were curators. Thus, we stuck together. We preserved. I opened up the bandwidth to include Ramin so we could talk three ways.

'Alright, Clio, you and I will walk the streets for a bit and see if we can spot anything. Ramin, track us, and keep an eye out on the police frequencies for any unusual activity.'

Was Julius already dead? I felt like I was wasting my time running up and down the streets, but what else could I do? If there was a chance that Julius was nearby, I couldn't walk away. I had told him he would be safe.

I scoured the streets gradually, becoming more and more anxious. I couldn't see him or Paul and was having to fight through throngs of wretched tourists with their phones out on sticks. No sooner had I broken free of them, than I would have to jump out of the way of a pod of cyclists all glaring at me. This was ridiculous. I was about to either throw a bike at the tourists or grab a selfie stick and hurl it between the spokes of a bike when I heard banging on a pane of glass. Snapping my head round, I saw Julius waving at me from the bay window of a café whilst sitting next to his sodding girlfriend. Was she the cause of his elevated heart rate? Had I been panicking for no good cause?

Relieved, I jogged across the road, leaving the cyclists and tourists to their relative safety, and headed into the café where it was immediately apparent that all was not well.

#31 Julius – Beta Earth

'Was that some sort of joke?' asked Rebecca, her voice shaky from suppressed tears.

'I don't know. Hang on in there.' Julius had been staring out of the window at the passers-by and saw Neith running along the other side of the road, looking left and right. He banged on the glass and was relieved to see her head whip in his direction. As she saw him she ran across, talking into her watch as she did so.

Leaning across the table, he gently held Rebecca's hand. 'It's okay, I think help is coming.'

'Julius, what's going on? Who was that man? Did he really have a gun?' Her voice was beginning to rise, but she stopped suddenly as Neith sat down at the table. Gathering her wits, she glared at Neith and then turned to Julius again. 'And who the hell is this?'

Ignoring Rebecca, Neith kept her eyes on Julius. 'Are you okay?' She was out of breath and her voice was laced with worry.

Julius paused. Could he trust her? What choice did he have?

'Your colleague just came in here and threatened to kill Rebecca if I didn't help him.'

'She knows him? This woman knows that thug?' Rebecca's voice was rising again. 'Julius, if you don't call the police I will.'

'They are the police, Rebecca, they're Special Branch.' Julius had no idea what they were, but it seemed to calm Rebecca's rising panic. Turning back to Neith, he too was scared and angry.

'So much for you having me under protection. He was going to shoot Rebecca and it looked like me as well.'

'Miss Greene, is your passport up to date?'

Rebecca nodded.

'I'm afraid Mr Strathclyde here has been helping us with our enquiries into the drive-by shooting of Charles Bradshaw. We hadn't anticipated a direct attempt on you, and for that, you have Her Majesty's Government's deepest apologies.'

The formal words began to sooth and reassure Rebecca.

'For operational reasons, we would like you out of the country so that you can't be used to threaten Julius again. Can you swing that at work?'

Rebecca nodded.

'Good. Take a friend. I'm transferring some money to your bank account and you can go wherever you want. In two days' time, this will all be resolved, but I'd feel happier knowing you were safe and out of the way. Do you fancy Hawaii?'

She muttered into her watch and then smiled at Rebecca. 'Please check your bank account.'

Rebecca pulled out her phone, and after a few clicks, she gasped at the screen.

'Good,' said Neith, 'that's enough money for you and a friend to have a lovely all-expenses-paid holiday in Hawaii. Or wherever you want to go. Your friend can travel with you now or join you later, but I need you on a plane as soon as possible. Do you agree?'

Rebecca just stared at her. 'Julius, what is all this? Are you safe?'

Julius smiled back. She was a nice person and didn't deserve all this drama.

'Rebecca, I'm so sorry. I really didn't want you caught up in this. I hardly know how I'm caught up in it all myself. It's something that Charlie was involved in. But I think they're right, I think a holiday would be a good idea.'

'But Charlie was murdered. What are you mixed up in?'

Julius sighed. 'Honestly, I have no idea, but I feel sick that you've been pulled into it.'

Neith spoke into her wrist piece and Clio walked into the café.

'Miss Greene. This is Special Agent Masoud. She's going to take you home to pack and will then drive you to Stansted Airport. If you tell her your final destination, she will get all the tickets and reservations sorted for you whilst you pack.'

Neith wondered where Clio had got the sunglasses from and liked the way she kept touching her ear. Every gesture portrayed her as a special agent and bodyguard.

Julius watched as Rebecca gradually started to calm down. 'I think you're right; I think a holiday is a good idea.' Turning to Julius, she looked at him with regret. 'And I also think you and I are over. I didn't sign up for this sort of thing at all. Good luck with your new friends.'

Pushing back her chair, she almost fled out of the café, causing nearby diners to stare curiously as Clio followed after her.

'I think we need to go as well,' said Neith. 'We're attracting too much attention.

'Is she going to be okay? Surely now that Paul has what he wants he won't go after her?'

Neith stared at him in horror. 'What do you mean Paul has what he wants?'

Julius squeezed his face between his hands, trying to release some of the tension that was still coursing through his body. 'The postcard. Charlie sent me a postcard with a cryptic message on the back. And now Paul has it. Your rogue operative has the only clue to the egg's location.'

#32 Sam – Alpha Earth

Chancellor Soliman flung the doors open and strode into the Step field control gantry. All heads turned to watch him, and Sam could swear that he could visibly see Soliman swell up just a little bit more. He wasn't certain that it was possible to be any more pompous or inflated, but there it was. Sam wandered in quietly behind him. An unkind person might have said *sidled*, but they wouldn't say it twice. The thing was, Sam knew how to enter a room and watch it working without anyone noticing. Pomp and circumstances were all very well, but they made it very hard to see what was going on. And Sam always liked to know exactly what was going on. Which, at this precise moment, was absolutely nothing, as all the technicians had stopped what they were doing and were waiting to see what their boss-on-high had to say.

'Back to work, everyone, pretend I'm not here. I've just come down to muck in with the troops.'

Turning back to Sam, he invited him to walk around the troops with him to "improve morale, show a steady hand".

Get completely in their way and slow them down, he thought.

As Soliman was asking one of the technicians how she managed to hold all those numbers in her head, it was all Sam could do to not roll his eyes. At least as he walked around with Soliman going from desk to desk, he knew who to apologise to later.

'Sir!'

The gate started flashing and everyone took a quantum pill from their pocket or desk. Sam always carried his on him but assumed Soliman didn't and offered him one of his.

'What's happening?'

'The gate is opening and someone's coming through. Quick, sir. The pill, it helps prevent nausea.'

Soliman surveyed the room. Everyone had taken their pills and was now getting into position. Conversation had dropped to a minimum and everyone was bracing themselves. Given that they were uncertain if the Q Field was in perfect working order, they were preparing for anything.

'No thanks, Sam, it's always important for the troops to see their leaders showing a bit of backbone. Did I tell you I once sailed single-handedly from the Red Sea to the tip of India? Didn't feed the fish once! I tell you…'

He stopped talking as the far wall started shimmering, and he threw up all over the desk in front of him, showing the troops exactly what he was made of and what he'd had for breakfast.

Engineers ran towards the wall with guns at the ready. Sam left the chancellor to it as he grabbed one of the spare guns and ran down the steps onto the main apron, standing ready to act with the others. He couldn't help himself. He missed the good old days of being down where the action was.

The Q Field engaged, and the world suddenly dissolved into memories of candyfloss and snow, of stars and pyramids. He was flying, he was drowning, he was laughing, and just as soon as it had started it stopped, and two people stepped through the gate as the wall behind them returned to a solid blank surface.

Both curators' clothes were heavily singed and there were still flames on one of their cuffs. Smiling, one of them held up a small book in his hands and the room burst into applause. Staff ran forward to put out the flames and medics ran past the soldiers to give the curators quick shots and initial burns treatment.

Sam waited until the pair had been assessed and then stepped forward, saluting both of them.

'Hello, sir,' said Johannes. 'Nice to receive a formal welcome. Was your desk boring you again? Are we doing debriefs down here now? I was looking forward to your little date cakes that you hide in your top drawer.'

Sam grinned. At least now he knew who was always nicking them. 'Debrief as normal. We've got a few things going on which I'll fill you in on after you've had a proper medical. But just quickly, did you notice any anomalies? Any gut feeling that something was wrong? Any problems with stepping through just now?'

Jo thought about it and looked at Diana. 'Nothing, sir. Perfectly straightforward. No issues beyond normal operational parameters and a smooth step. What's wrong?'

'I'll explain later, but go and get treated first.'

As the pair left the room with the medics, Sam turned to Farnaz. 'One mission down, two to go. I tell you, I won't be happy until they are all back and we can then try to work out what the hell's been happening.'

Sam had returned to the gantry and was leaning on the console, taking in the readings from this Step. Everything looked perfect. If he hadn't seen it for himself, he wouldn't have known that, hours earlier, the Q Field had been having some sort of seizure. Now, to all intents and purposes, it was whistling sweetly, toeing its foot in the sand and asking, "Who me?"

Soliman had joined the two of them. No one mentioned the earlier loss of stomach control, studiously avoiding each other's eyes. In the far corner, a technician was looking at his work desk in horror.

'Are you sure there's a problem with the gate? These readings appear perfect to me. That team said nothing was wrong.' Soliman looked around the room with a mild avuncular air. 'I wonder if maybe you're all jumping at shadows?'

Sam grimaced. It was bad form to not know the names of the two curators that had just stepped through the gate. It was bad form to criticise the operations team in front of them. It was bad form to undermine Sam's authority in front of said team, but the biggest breach of etiquette was to do it all with vomit on your sleeve.

'Sir. Believe me, there is a problem. Johannes and Diana have reported one situation. I personally witnessed a second. And whilst I still have two retrieval teams out in the field, I will be jumping at all the shadows until they're home.'

Soliman bristled and was prepared to take Sam to task; it was one thing to be unprofessional in private, but here in front of the staff it was unacceptable. Just as he took in a deep breath, a voice cut across him.

'Clearly it wasn't their angel then.'

All three turned to look at the engineer.

'Angel?' asked Farnaz.

As the man was about to reply, Soliman jumped in. 'Protocols, man! We do not discuss angels whilst an incident is on-going.'

'No, wait though. Excuse me, sir,' said Farnaz. 'You are, of course, completely correct, but there hasn't been an angel incident. Sam?'

Sam looked just as confused. All angel incidents were sent straight to him. If an angel had come through on another shift, Farnaz may not necessarily know about it, but Sam would. And as an act of professional courtesy, he would have informed all shift heads of any events that would affect their routine. Angels were treated as classified events, but in reality, they were pretty much open knowledge within the Step room, regardless of which shift they occurred on.

'Jim, why did you mention an angel?'

'Because of the one that came through the other day?' Jim's face was waxy. He knew the protocol was to not talk about them, but what with the two recent incidents and an angel, he had assumed that everyone would be talking about nothing else. Now the chancellor was glaring at him, and he wondered if he would have a job in the morning.

'There was no angel,' said Sam.

'Yesterday one stepped through on the evening shift. I heard about it from one of the team.'

'You mean gossiping,' snapped Soliman, turning to Sam. 'Is this the sort of discipline that you think leads to an effective task force? One false alarm and they start wittering like little birds on the acacia trees?'

'I will remind the teams about protocols, but at the moment we have a bigger problem.'

'And what would that be, exactly?'

'Where is the angel?'

#33 Neith – Beta Earth

As we got out of the taxi, the front door opened, and I bundled Julius into the house before Ramin bolted the door behind us.

'Are the perimeters secured? New passwords?'

When Ramin confirmed that they were, I relaxed a tad. 'You were right, Paul's gone rogue, but I don't understand why.'

Before I could do any more, I went and double-checked the security for myself. And then, only when I was happy that we were as secure as could be, I returned to the front room and stood by the fire. Julius was perched on the edge of an armchair. Ramin was sitting in another armchair, his head hanging in his hands.

'So, what did you discover? What the hell has happened?'

My oldest friend looked every one of his years as he turned to me. When he looked up, I was horrified to see he was close to tears.

'This is my fault. I didn't believe him,' he said and gestured at Julius.

'Claws, I'm so sorry, mate. I should have trusted you to know what you were witnessing.'

Julius shrugged. 'It's okay. I guess you were more likely to trust a friend over a stranger.'

I coughed. 'If you too have finished bonding, maybe one of you would like to let me know what's going on?'

And for the second time, I got sucker-punched.

'What do you mean? It was Paul who hit me!' I turned to Ramin as Julius explained what he had seen. 'And you knew? Are you fucking kidding me?'

'I don't know what to say. I just didn't trust him. And when I told him he'd been mistaken, he agreed with me.'

'Of course he did! He was probably terrified that you might attack him.'

'I would never—'

'*He* doesn't know that!'

I was shaking so hard that I didn't know what to say. 'Can I speak?'

I looked at Julius, who seemed calm. Certainly calmer than me or Ramin. I took a deep breath. Why not? Why not listen to some wet behind the ears, know nothing Beta? He couldn't do worse than we apparently had.

'The way I see it, you are on some sort of self-imposed deadline. Why don't you just call your boss and explain the defection? Call for re-enforcements.'

'The deadline is fixed. By Wednesday we're going home, with or without the egg. And we don't get back-up. All we can do is report problems; if we screw up, we have to fix it or abort. No one is coming to save the day.'

Julius interrupted her. 'So, you're isolated, and you can't trust your team?' Julius didn't wait for Neith to agree and ignored Ramin's protest. 'You want the egg and I want whoever killed my friend to be put behind bars. Was it Paul who killed Charlie?'

'No!'

'Any proof of that?'

'He wouldn't.'

'Honestly, Neith, you seem like a smart person and a born leader, but you're not thinking clearly. When we last met, you said you suspected another team was working against you. I say it was Paul. And he clearly wasn't working alone. I told Ramin here what was going on and he failed to tell you. Clio hit me hard enough to damn near kill me. What sort of team are you running?'

'Enough!' snapped Ramin. 'I would *never* betray Neith.'

I smiled at him. He didn't need to say that. I would trust him with my life. Him and Clio. That said, two hours ago I'd have trusted Paul with my life as well. I was compromised. The whole team was, and I needed to fix things quickly. But first I wanted to try to understand Julius' calm.

'You seem remarkably relaxed? You have been the target of a second kidnap attempt, had a gun aimed at you, and you've lost your girlfriend. Why aren't you a gibbering wreck?'

He looked at me and shrugged, a wry smile on his face. 'No idea. But this is a puzzle, and I'm good at those. I can't do anything about the stuff that you mentioned. That's in the past, all done and dusted. But here and now is a problem, a situation that needs fixing, and that is something that I *can* do. No doubt I'll have a full-on meltdown soon, but for now, I'm intrigued.' He shrugged again and I smiled back at him.

'That's the spirit. Right, Ramin. Tell me, what else did you discover when you were examining Paul's case notes?'

'I found missing files, lots of blanks. So, I went back to the beginning. I looked up the police report regarding the death of Zofia Guskov; her body was only found a week ago. Neighbours were worried that they hadn't seen her for a few days. The story that Paul told us was a pack of lies.' Ramin ran his hand through his hair, messing it up. 'When you asked him to check the CCTV cameras of the drive-by shooting? He didn't. So, I did, half an hour ago. And I could see that the footage had been expertly edited. There are lots of little things like that. On reflection, I can only conclude that Paul was working with the assassins. He didn't miss the car. He was actively helping them. Same as when he was charged with covering the exit at the church. He saw them, of course, he did. He set us all up. He knew where we were going and set up the ambush. When you were winning the fight, he took you out. And as Julius here saw, the rest of the team stopped fighting straightaway. They had failed to grab Julius as Clio had got him to safety.'

I could barely take it all in. If what Ramin said was correct then Paul may have killed Zofia and been actively trying to steal the egg ever since we arrived.

Ramin turned to Julius. 'You should thank Clio for saving your life by the way, when you next see her. Not cast aspersions her way.'

Julius snorted. And I felt a touch of sympathy. Having your life saved by Clio could sometimes be bruising. Thinking of her, I gave her a quick call, whilst I tried to process Ramin's report.

'Sitrep please.'

'Hey, beautiful. All good at our end. Hang on, Rebecca, wave at the screen.'

Next minute Rebecca was smiling cautiously at the screen.

'Rebecca, are you okay?'

'Yes, Julius, I am. I'm sorry about cutting and running, but this is just not my thing. We're pulling into Stansted now. I've got to go.'

The screen cut off. 'Well, she seems to have bounced back quickly,' said Neith.

Julius left out a deep breath. 'Good. I'm glad she's safe. Now, let's get that egg and get you out of Cambridge, and out of my bloody life.'

I looked at him thoughtfully. He was still a bit too calm for my liking.

'Is there something you know that I don't?'

'I should imagine there's quite a lot. But as pertains to the egg, I know how to find it.'

'What!' shouted Ramin, saving me from having to do it myself. Instead, I tried to keep my temper.

'When were you planning on telling me this?'

'When I knew Rebecca was safe.'

'Well. Go on. Where is it?'

He shrugged his shoulders. 'I don't know.'

'Oh, may great Bast preserve me. In the name of all that you hold dear, what the hell are you blithering on about?'

I may have lost my cool, but Julius just looked at me from beneath a raised eyebrow. He appeared utterly unfazed by my reaction.

'He wrote the clue on the back of a postcard. Paul may have the postcard, but I bet he doesn't know what it means.'

'Why?'

'Because I don't either.'

I stared at the ceiling and counted to ten. Then I counted to twenty. Then I took a deep breath and tried again.

'Okay. What did it say?'

Julius looked at Ramin, then back at me, and shook his head.

'No. I don't trust him, and I don't trust Clio. The only person so far that has behaved in any way trustworthy or honourably is you. I will tell you only. And not here. This house could be bugged.'

'This is the safest spot for you right now.'

'If you'll forgive me, nowhere near you lot feels very safe right now.'

I pinched my nose. 'Do you honestly think you could fight Paul off on his own? Or the thugs he has hired? Or whoever his boss is? At least here you know whose side we are on.'

Ramin coughed.

'She's right, you know. And we are a team. I would never let her down. Paul's betrayal has rocked us to our core, but we're still your best option for protection. If you want, I can move to another section of the house. But understand this, if Paul is out there trying to grab the egg then I will give my last breath to protect Neith. I won't let your suspicions of me get in the way of that. Am I clear?'

#34 Sam – Alpha Earth

Sam and Soliman headed to the infirmary. An unreported angel event was unheard of. He had already put in wake-up calls to all the staff on that shift, but, in the meantime, he could try to establish where the angel had come from. Jo and Di were currently going through their scrub-down as Sam went over to them. He had already ruled them out as it would have been the first thing they mentioned, but he needed to be certain.

Returning to Soliman, he confirmed that they hadn't sent an angel. Soliman then shouted at an orderly to summon the head of the infirmary immediately. Alarmed by the raised voice in the hospital ward, a member of staff dashed out from behind a desk. She could hardly tell the chancellor to be quiet, but she did try to explain that Dr Giovanetti was currently supervising intern operations.

'I don't care if they've got their arm halfway up a cadaver's arse. Get them here now,' roared Soliman, as Sam winced on behalf of cadavers everywhere.

As they waited, Sam had to listen to Soliman tearing strips off him. He was losing his grip. The team were sloppy and making up stories, no doubt to cover their own ineptitudes. Orderlies and nurses crept around the two men, closing bedroom doors to try to lessen the noise. Sam stood silent as his boss raged, but inwardly he relaxed as he saw Haru striding down the corridor.

Sam was delighted to see the fury on his old friend's face. Here in the infirmary, only one voice mattered, and it was not the one currently shouting and blustering.

'Gentlemen. My office please. And keep your voices down. This is a hospital, not a playground.'

'Dr Giovanetti—'

'Chancellor. This is my hospital. If you have an issue with how I run it take it up with your bosses.' Turning on his heel, he walked off down the corridor toward his office. The chancellor may have technically outranked him, but when it came to the chain of command both men were section heads and reported to the local civil agency headed up by Director Ranai al-Cavifi. If they wanted to play turf wars it would be down to her to break it up.

Sam followed quickly, keeping his face as neutral as possible. If Soliman couldn't reprimand Haru, he could totally bollock Sam, and from the set of his jaw, Sam knew his boss was furious. As the three men settled into Haru's office, Soliman launched into an offensive line of attack.

'When did you last have an angel incident?'

Haru looked at him with mild surprise. 'Through the Q Field or one back for routine treatment?'

'Q Field,' barked Soliman, as though it were obvious which he had wanted.

'About six months ago. I'll have to check the logs for the exact date.'

'Not yesterday then?'

Haru cocked his head. 'No, of course not.'

Soliman turned to Sam. 'Captain Nymens, I want a full report on my desk in an hour about the ridiculous way your team has been proceeding. After that, you can go home whilst I try to sort out this shambolic mess you've left your department in.' And with that he stormed out, leaving Haru looking shocked and Sam looking thoughtful.

'Sorry about that.'

'Sam, what the hell is going on?'

'Nothing good. Can you do me a favour? Can you privately ask Asha to come to my office immediately? Ask her to do it unofficially.'

Asha was Haru's wife and head of security. The pair were a bit of a dream team and had been since college. Eschewing children, they had put all their energies into their relationship and their departments. Asha would laugh that it was a typical husband and wife team. He would go around after her, patching things up. In truth, she often followed where he led, and as a pair, they had developed strategies for saving lives both on and off the field of conflict.

'Of course I can, but what's all this about an angel?'

Sam went on to explain about the strange reading from the Q Field and a reported angel event but left it at that. He didn't want to compromise him.

'I don't know what's happening, Haru, I just know that something is very wrong, and I still have six of my team out there. If they did send an angel, they're in trouble. Plus, we have a missing angel. If no one sent an angel, I have a shift that's lying. And now I have a boss that's trying to stop my investigation. Like I said, something stinks.'

Sam headed back to his office and was unsurprised to find Asha already waiting for him. Haru had already filled her in on what he had witnessed, and Asha was concerned. Her chain of command was clear. She reported to Soliman, but Sam was a friend. As yet she had received no orders regarding his position, so for now she decided to hear him out, without compromising any protocols.

'Hi, Asha. Can you pull up footage from the security cameras for the other day? And can you do it so that no one sees what you're doing?'

She raised an eyebrow but accessed a keyboard, and after a few keystrokes asked what timeframe he wanted to look at. For a few minutes, they both watched the footage as it sped through the night.

'Nothing.' Sam sighed and put his head in his hands. 'Why would they lie?'

'Why would who lie, Sam? Haru hasn't told me what's going on, just that you needed help immediately. So, what's up?'

Sam went on to explain again and realised that each time he tried to mention a disappearing angel he heard how ridiculous it sounded. The security breach would be monumental. And now here he was, trying to explain just such a situation to the person in charge of it. Thank

Ra they were old mates, though he suspected he might be pushing the limits of that friendship.

'Sam, do you know how damn near impossible what you're saying is?'

'I know. Forget it. I'm just wound up. The Q Field isn't working properly, there've been problems with some of the artefact storage and, oh, I don't know…' Sam leant back in his chair and exhaled noisily. 'Something's just not right, and it's bugging me.'

Asha watched him thoughtfully. She was insulted that he had cast aspersions on her systems. The thing was though, that she too had been noticing tiny oddities, and until Sam vocalised it, she hadn't realised how on edge she was too.

She pulled the keyboard towards her again and spent a longer time running through a chain of keystrokes. Once she was happy with her subroutine, she hit send. Once more, footage from the night before spun up, only this time the wall could be very clearly seen to pulse and shimmer. A frail old woman stepped through as soldiers and medics stood ready. One of the medics helped the old woman and, retrieving a wheelchair, wheeled her out of the room and into the outer corridor.

'What the hell was that?' asked Sam.

'Well, I'd say that was your angel. And evidence that someone has tampered with the system. I've always kept a private back-up. Call me paranoid.'

'I just call you head of security, but I think that's the same thing.'

'Okay, let's see what happened next.'

Asha hit the keyboard again and added the exact timeframe into the security footage for the corridors. The door opened as the medic and the old lady left the Q Zone. As the door closed behind them, Asha and Sam watched as the man wheeled the angel along the empty corridor then without warning the screen went black.

'Blast!'

'What's happened?'

'Your medic has pulsed the security cameras. The way I see it, they couldn't risk pulsing the cameras in the Q Field, as that would raise alarms. They waited until they were in the corridor, then discharged a localised EMP to knock out the cameras.'

'But—'

'Hang on, Sam, I'm thinking.'

There was a pause as Asha closed her eyes. When she opened them again, she looked worried. 'We have a serious problem. More than one person's involved. At least someone in security, to have doctored the tapes and thrown a veil over an EM pulse. That would've been noted, but someone scrubbed it. The medic there is definitely involved in whatever is going on. And someone wanted to buy time and may have already done what they wanted to achieve. News of the angel's disappearance would have been inescapable by the time that shift came back to work. Something has happened. Sam, I need to report this.'

'Agreed. You also need to track down that medic.'

As they stood up the sirens went off, and Asha's comms badge pinged. Patching the call through, she nodded, saying she was on her way and to secure the area. She turned to Sam, her face hard.

'Well, we've found the medic. But we won't be able to question him. He's been murdered.'

Asha and Sam hurried toward the main atrium. The Library of Alexandria was not just a Research Facility, it was also a world-famous tourist attraction. Home to the famous collection of Beta artefacts and the planet's only Q Field, it was a place of veneration, as well as wonder. Added to which, it was a fifty-acre campus covered in beautiful sections of formal lawns and gardens as they sloped gently down to the banks of Lake Mareotis on one side, and the Mediterranean Sea on the other. Families would picnic and play by the water's edge. Researchers would come from across the globe to Alexandria, the cultural capital of Africa, and the library complex was its crown jewel.

By the time they got to the corridor, the area was full of tourists. Some were openly crying, others were standing around shaking, scared, and hugging each other. A cleaner was sitting on the ground being treated by two pale-faced orderlies. Shoved into a broom cupboard sat a very dead medic. The green tinge to his skin, as well as the stench and the flies, very clearly spoke to his deceased status, as did the obviously broken neck.

As extra guards arrived, Asha had the corridors cleared of bystanders. As they walked past Sam he heard the same snippets of conversation around him. How it had to be a Beta. Someone had jumped through, escaped. Everyone knew Betas were irrational blood-soaked crazies.

In fairness their shock was understandable. Violent crime was low on Alpha. It wasn't absent, by any means, but it was certainly a safer, more stable world than that of Beta Earth. The odd flare up always happened, but with far more equitable societies and fewer territorial disputes, outbreaks of violence were lessened.

All Alphas knew that this wasn't the case on Beta Earth. They lapped up their culture with voyeuristic glee. The killings, the wars, the thefts, the punishments; all of these things were alarming and exciting and safely experienced through films and books. Now, here was a genuine act of violence in the heart of their cultural icon.

Sam snorted. Privately, the idea that a six-foot medic had been taken out by an elderly, disease-riddled Beta, was ludicrous. Still, the general public didn't know there was an unaccounted for angel roaming around. No need to alarm them unnecessarily.

Soliman's voice boomed across the atrium. 'No need to panic. My operatives will soon apprehend the fugitive Beta individual. Your security is my primary concern.'

Sam was not alone in taking in a gulp of air and clenching his teeth. No one had mentioned a missing Beta individual. It was just gossip and wild rumour. That was until Soliman publicly declared it. Sam watched as a wave of horror swept across the tourists' faces and the panic began to mount.

'Oh, so you do believe in the angel now then?' Sam couldn't contain his sarcasm.

'Asha brought me up to speed as I came over. Have you submitted your report yet?'

'The report on the fictitious event which turns out to have happened? Or the lack of discipline in my team that actually alerted us to a crime? Or did you mean the report on the general sloppiness of my department that has just revealed a major cover-up? Which report was it, sir?'

'I should fire you right now for insubordination!'

'Sir, respectfully.' Asha pulled Soliman to one side and after a few minutes, Soliman gave Sam a curt nod. 'I want a full report on all operating procedures on my desk by the end of the day. I want your observations on what is wrong with the Q Field, the current status of the two remaining teams, and how one of your medics got themselves killed by a little old lady!' His voice rose to a crescendo as he roared his instructions at Sam. Walking over to the cordon, where various camera crews were converging, he began to do what he was best at. Talking to the camera and letting everyone know that he was in charge.

Sam pinched his nose and turned to Asha. 'How did you pull that off?'

'Told him you were up to your neck in it and it was better to have you inside the tent where I could keep an eye on you.'

'Keep your friends close, hey?'

'Exactly, but I would just say it's curious the speed with which Soliman has tried to remove you from the investigation.'

There was a commotion from the perimeter, and Sam saw Farnaz trying to get through. She was holding tightly onto a young medic's arm, who was visibly distressed. He looked at his watch and realised that her shift had already ended. Nodding to Asha, she waved Farnaz and the medic past the guards.

'Sir, Chief, I heard about this event as the shift was ending so I brought Janet here for protection and/or interrogation.'

Sam was puzzled, but Asha cottoned on immediately and summoned two guards to take the trembling medic to a secure room. No one was to enter until she joined them.

'What have I missed?'

'Not what, Sam, *when*. Someone was clearly anticipating that an angel might come through. That means that whatever is happening on the other side, someone on this side knows about it and knows that the team might be in distress.'

Sam nodded. That made sense but painted an even more serious incident. 'You said "when"?'

'Yes, whoever this is had no way of knowing if an angel was coming through or when that might be, so they had to get to the on-call medic for each shift. We need the name of the medic on the third shift. Let's go and pick them up, and see what they and Miss Janet have to say for themselves.'

She turned and smiled at Farnaz. 'Good work. Any time you want to join security I'll sign you straight through.' Turning back to Sam, she looked more concerned. 'I think the angel is dead as well, but just in case I'm wrong we'll do all we can to find her and get her to safety.'

Both reflected on how terrifying this experience would be to a sick and confused Beta. Sam nodded. The day had started poorly and was just getting worse.

'I'll be at the Q Zone until all the teams are back. Can you brief me, as well as my Glorious Leader over there, with any findings you get? You know, just in case he forgets to tell me?'

As he reached the cordon on the other side of the plaza, Asha caught up with him.

'Sam, I didn't want to say this where I could be overheard, but someone on our side murdered that medic. Please be really careful. I wouldn't normally recommend this, but maybe carry your stunner with you at all times until I've arrested those involved.'

Sam agreed and headed back to the Q Field. There was no need to say that he had been carrying his gun ever since the first anomaly on the gate was reported.

Interlude 4

The following text conversation was retrieved, doing a sweep of the ghost files of the Q Zone security system. It has been added to the evidence report for Case No: 234530/H. As yet neither correspondent has been identified.

- Are you an idiot?

- What?

- Killing the medic. On the actual plaza. You've drawn the attention of

  every single person on the globe. A murder at the Mouseion of Alexandria.

- I had to take care of the angel. They could have talked.

- They're not talking though, are they? But the rest of the bloody world is!

- That's hardly my problem.

- Again, I do not appreciate your tone. If you are incapable of securing that egg for us, there will be repercussions. Noticeable ones. Unpleasant ones.

- Am I clear?

- Crystal.

#35 Julius – Beta Earth

Julius had endured a rotten night's sleep. The place was a sauna; he didn't know much about these people, but he had decided they all had a problem with temperature control. The heating had been on full whack all night, so he'd had to sleep with the windows open as well as on top of the sheets, having kicked the duvet and blankets, to the floor. He'd been tempted to sleep in the buff, but that just felt a bit too vulnerable given all the recent events. If he were going to be attacked by unknown assailants, he would resist in more than his altogether. It felt a bit grubby sleeping in his boxers, but at least he would maintain a modicum of dignity whilst fleeing for his life. Plus, he had a feeling Neith might laugh.

Whilst he had lain in bed thinking about Neith, he tried to think if he could do anything to impress her. Beyond running quickly away from bad guys in his boxer shorts. He knew he was trying to show off, which made him ponder. She was certainly an interesting individual, if a little unconventional. He had a limited skill set; he wasn't a martial arts expert or a cage fighter or a tracker, but Neith, Clio and Ramin seemed to have those skills covered. What he was, was a brilliant researcher. Admittedly, those three seemed to be that as well, but he did have a few advantages over them. The first was that they didn't appear to be locals, so he would know stuff that just didn't turn up on the internet. The second was that he was Charlie's oldest friend, which meant he knew stuff that no one else did. He didn't know if that was going to help, but it just might. Getting up, he washed and headed for the kitchen. The fire was already lit in the living room, and the three of them were almost sat on top of it eating breakfast. Julius made a coffee and, having said good morning, went and sat in the garden. The cold, crisp air filled his lungs and he watched as a robin was giving its all in the early morning sunshine.

After a bit, Ramin came and joined him.

'Too hot for you as well?' Julius said and smiled. He was trying to build bridges with Neith's team, so he may as well start with Ramin; of the two of them, he seemed less full of psychotic malevolence. He was sure Clio was a lovely girl and that she meant well, but he and his lungs were still a bit skittish around her. At least Ramin, to date, had not tried to put him in hospital.

'Not quite,' said Ramin, who was looking decidedly shivery, 'but we can't protect you out here. It's unlikely that Paul would attempt a snatch from the grounds, but we can't risk it, so I said I'd come and keep you company.'

'How are you doing?' Julius asked and Ramin looked at him in surprise. Julius continued. 'Paul was clearly a friend. This defection must be a terrible shock?'

Ramin paused and Julius saw that he was battling to try and control his emotions. He suddenly felt contrite, this man had probably saved his life and now he was struggling to come to terms with a painful betrayal, whilst shivering in the garden, just so that Julius could sit outside. Despite Ramin's protests, he headed back indoors. He couldn't bear the idea of someone suffering whilst trying to save his life. Plus, the appeal of fresh air had suddenly waned.

'Close the sodding door!' shouted one of the girls from the living room, and whilst Julius wasn't sure which one it was, he took no chances and shut it quickly.

Walking through to join them, he asked if anyone would like another cup of coffee. 'Also, can I log on to one of the laptops in the dining room?'

The dining room appeared to have been turned into a workstation and had several laptops. Various screens were monitoring security cameras, and lines of text were constantly updating on another. He wasn't completely au fait with the local police intelligentsia, but he wondered if they knew how easily their system could be hacked. 'I'd like to start researching the clue, but I don't want to interrupt any of your feeds.'

If these guys were above board, this would be the moment when one of them would jump in. They would reassure him that they had permission for all these surveillance hacks, or it wasn't what it seemed, or it was, but that wasn't what was important right now. The silence, however, was deafening. He was so tempted to walk away but currently, he had a rogue man with a gun after him and a dead best friend. A best friend who had sent him his final message. Meaning, he was stuck with these guys until the egg or the assailant was found. He didn't much care which one came first. The egg hunt had been fun, right up until the shooting had started. Since then, life had been pretty scary.

'I'll make the coffees,' said Clio. 'Least I can do to make amends. Ramin, set him up on a laptop and let's see if the three of us can't work out what your friend was trying to tell you.'

Clio surprised him with a genuinely apologetic smile as she headed off for the kitchen. He joined Ramin and Neith in the dining room.

'Told you she isn't that scary.' Ramin set Julius up with a spare laptop, and soon the four of them were scanning through various pages, searching for correlations.

Franklin's hungry. Look up Lucky. They must have said the phrase a hundred times, but still nothing seemed to be springing to mind.

'And you're sure about the spelling and the punctuation?' asked Clio.

'I'm not going to swear on it, but I think so. But maybe there was more to it? Maybe Charlie had hidden an extra clue under the stamp. Maybe there was something in the picture on the front. I didn't give it that much of an examination.'

'Might have helped if you had,' drawled Clio.

'Might have helped if you didn't hire traitors.'

The four of them subsided into sullen silence. Julius knew Charlie's parents lived in the States. Maybe there was a connection to Benjamin Franklin. But he was damned if he could find it.

At one point Julius glanced over at Ramin's screen and was mesmerised by an unfamiliar search engine that appeared to be making massive leaps across various platforms, spotting nodes all across the internet.

'What the hell is that?' Looking back at Google, Julius felt distinctly envious.

'Tiresias. It's a new search engine in Beta mode. I'd log you in, but it takes a while to learn.'

'I'm a quick learner.'

Ramin laughed. 'I'm sure you are, but I meant Tiresias is a slow learner. It needs about fifty search hours of your browsing behaviour before it adapts and finds what you're looking for. It's an intuitive engine. The more you use it, the better it understands how you think and helps make the leaps for you.'

Julius' jaw dropped. That sounded incredible, and he hit Google for early Beta versions of it, but came up blank.

'Is it spelt Tiresias, like the blind Greek seer?'

'Yes, but don't bother trying to find it. This is completely off the grid.'

Julius glared into his coffee and returned to the keyboard. As the hours passed, he became more engrossed in various leads, but nothing seemed to be making sense. He was aware of Neith working alongside him, but her concentration was also fixed on the screen. As well as trying to break the clue, the other three were trying to see if the egg had surfaced anywhere, or if they could track the location of Paul.

Ramin pushed back from the table to put the kettle on, wondering if they were actually going to fail on this mission. He wouldn't be surprised. Having a teammate go rogue was bound to put a spanner in the works. Clio was already in the kitchen eating a bowl of rice and veg, and the smell reminded him how hungry he was.

'Any left?' He grabbed a bowl and took a few heavenly mouthfuls, then gently waved his fork in Julius' direction.

'I don't know if I trust him.'

'Good!'

'You don't trust him either?'

'No, I mean you shouldn't just randomly trust people. Look where it's got us so far. Your teammate has turned on us and is implicated in the murder of two shit flies so far. You trusted him, didn't you?'

Clio was being an arse, but she wasn't wrong. He loathed the implication that he was guilty by association, but he was, and he couldn't blame Clio for being hyper-vigilant. He liked Julius, but at this stage, he no longer knew whom to trust. It was inconceivable that he was working with anyone from the Alpha planet, but maybe he was trying to grab the egg for himself?

'Penny for them?'

'Well, I was just thinking that it was impossible for him to be working with someone from home. But what if it's not impossible?'

'You think there are Alpha operatives living here on Beta?' She could barely keep the incredulity out of her voice. 'And they just happened to be stationed at the right time and location? Or did you think someone snuck through the stepper whilst everyone else's backs were turned?' She snorted. 'There isn't a second team here. For some reason, Paul has gone rogue.'

'Well, don't you think "just gone rogue" is a bit too simplistic? He clearly has help. How did he arrange that?'

'Yes, because manipulating a bunch of shit flies to do his bidding is going to be so difficult. Crocs' sake, even a first-year Alpha could manage that.'

Ramin was worried. Clio wasn't wrong, but this didn't add up.

'Or maybe he did have help. Inside help?' She looked at him in an accusing fashion.

'For fuck's sake, Clio, trying to pin the blame on me isn't going to help anyone. Why don't you get back to the screens and see if you can track any unusual activity? Beyond friends stabbing each other in the back.'

'Whatever. I'm having a bath.'

Ramin waited until his temper had calmed down, and then walked through to the dining room. Neith and Julius had their backs to him, both engrossed in their respective screens. As he watched, Neith absentmindedly stretched out her left hand, looking for something to write with, whilst she continued to monitor the laptop. Without moving his head from his screen, Julius picked up the pencil and passed it to her. Bizarrely, that little act of cohesion made Ramin suddenly warm to Julius. It was a gesture that he had made himself a thousand times, and yet only people who were dedicated researchers seemed to have that symbiosis. It didn't matter that he was a Beta and may also be a baddie. He was patently one of them.

'Any joy?'

Both stopped what they were doing and turned to look at him.

'Not even bugger all,' said Julius, looking defeated. He had woken this morning determined to crack the clue but had ended up being sucked down a rabbit hole of interesting but ultimately useless bits of trivia.

'Okay. I think I have the solution. It occurs to me that Julius needs to do Tiresias old school.'

Julius perked up. 'What did you have in mind, and what do you mean by "old school"?'

'Tiresias is an intuitive engine, but you already have the prototype intuitive engine. You just need to feed it some data. *Mens sana in corpore sano*.'

Ramin was gratified when Neith finally laughed. She jumped up and grabbed him, kissing him firmly on the lips.

'Would someone care to fill me in?'

'Sorry, Julius,' said Ramin, 'it's this,' he added as he tapped his head. 'Your brain is the best intuition engine there is. A Tiresias simply amplifies it, but we can still do this without one. We need to get you tuned in. You need to go and hang out in places that remind you of Charles, sorry, Charlie, and you need to be well fed and relaxed. Once you're in an optimal state of mind, ideas will start jumping out at you.'

'First things first,' said Neith, looking at Julius, 'if you and I are heading out I'd be much happier if we could place a tracker on you. Do I have your consent? We all have one so we can track each other. Of course, Paul has switched his off.'

Julius thought this was a good idea and handed over his phone.

'No, this would be under your skin, so it can't be lost or removed.'

'Does it hurt?'

'Not in the slightest. Is that a yes? You'll be much safer if we know where you are at all times.'

Julius was cautious, but as Neith stuck her hand out, he couldn't help but shake it. The minute he had, she declared that it was all done and nodded at Ramin, who was busy typing away on a keyboard.

'Just like that?' Julius turned his hand over and compared it with his other, but couldn't see or feel any difference. Worried that he might begin to obsess over their subterfuge, she grabbed their coats and hurried him out the door.

'When Clio gets out of the bath, let her know what we're doing. Also, tell her I've got her coat. And please, Level Four protocols.'

As they left, Ramin could hear Neith muttering about the weather and he saw with dismay that it had started to snow again. She'd kill him when she got back if this didn't produce results. Clearing up the cups, he sat down at the keyboard and continued to search for any anomalies that might point to Paul.

'Where are the others?' Clio stood in a long dressing gown, her skin pink from having been scalded in a hot bath.

'Nipped into Julius' work. He said he wanted to show his face. Let everyone know that nothing odd was happening.'

'What the fuck? Why didn't Neith run it past me first? So much for Level Four protocols. At least tell me they switched on Julius' tracker again?'

'He refused. Said it was invasive.'

'She asked him? What's wrong with her? She should have just pinged him again without his permission.'

'I know that, but you know how ethical she gets about Betas. Now that he's living with us, he's practically a guest.'

Clio balled her hair up in her fists. Nothing about this assignment was going right, and she had a bad feeling it was about to get a whole lot worse.

#36 Neith – Beta Earth

I was finally beginning to get a good feeling about this mission. Admittedly, in the whole human endeavour of shitshows, this was beginning to stack up, but so far only two people were dead, no plagues had erupted, and no buildings had burnt down. Plus, the artefact wasn't yet lost to eternity. So, on the whole, things were looking up.

I was also enjoying Julius' company; he had a sharp wit and shunned prattle. A fine fellow in every aspect.

'When you shook my hand that was bullshit wasn't it?'

I didn't mind a fine mind, but it was annoying when they were quick. It was so much harder to pull the wool over their eyes. I tried to offer him some flannel, but he was having none of it.

'Don't lie. I've been thinking about it.' He didn't sound mad, just stubborn. 'You've already placed a tracker on me, haven't you? You just re-activated it. There's no way you could have broken my skin without hurting me and you had no time to apply an analgesic. Admit it.'

He was standing still, challenging me. I needed to understand the clue to the egg, and I needed him to pull himself together. I ran through a few scenarios and decided that the quickest and most effective would be the truth. Some of it.

'Yes. We tagged you after the funeral. You have a tracker under your skin, near where Clio kicked you. Ramin installed it when he was helping to tend your wound.'

'Is that how you got to me so quickly when Paul grabbed me and Rebecca?'

'Yes.' I waited to see if the truth was going to work for me or against. 'But, when he grabbed you, he ran a scanner over you that deactivated it. We'd have been with you much quicker if he hadn't. We only had your last location to go from. The minute it switched off, we came running. We knew something had gone wrong, just not what.'

'Like, if I was dead?'

'Oh no, we'd know that. Just because you die, the tracker doesn't stop transmitting. How would we know where to find the body, silly?'

Julius didn't seem impressed with my light-hearted tone, so I tried to reassure him by telling him how accurate it was. This appeared to backfire.

'So, you can tell my emotional state by monitoring my blood chemistry?'

Now he sounded pissed off.

'Focus, Julius. It saved your life. Later on, if we survive this, I'll show you how it works.'

I couldn't help but grin. He was instantly mollified. Ethics be damned, Julius just wanted to get to the bottom of things.

'Okay, illegal spy technology aside, let's go feed my intuition engine. I'd recommend the market for some street food, but I reckon you need somewhere warm, so let's go to The Eagle. It's one of our old haunts.'

The pub was warm and buzzing, and we stamped the snow off our boots and headed to the bar. I was pleased to see Julius order a pint of stout, and I made him laugh when I said I'd have the same with a cherry on top. He and the barman shared a look, which women the two worlds over have had to endure since the dawn of time, but it made me smile. I knew I should be on high alert, and I was, but it was reassuring to see Julius relaxing. If I could allow him to indulge in a spot of male camaraderie, then so much the better.

Julius had also ordered a plate of chips, and as we tucked into them, I asked him about the clues.

'So, *Franklin's hungry*. This entire clue was meant for you alone. Something you and he both knew intimately. He was confident enough that you would understand the clue, so what does it mean?' I ignored Julius' frown. I was spitballing, and I didn't expect him to instantly crack it. I just wanted to start some associations while he was in a relaxed and familiar space. 'Ben Franklin? Aretha Franklin? Franklin Mill? Have you ever been to America? Benjamin Franklin was a Freemason? Was Charlie?'

'Oh, Freemasons! I hadn't thought of that avenue.'

'Was Charlie a Freemason? Is that the first clue? Did the pair of you have a joke about Freemasons?

242

Something like that.' I was excited, and I felt we were close to something. Freemasons always seemed to provide the clues to any damn thing.

'No, not that I know of. Just an interesting thread I hadn't thought of.'

I gritted my teeth. I needed Julius to free associate and wander, but I really would have preferred it if he could just free-associate with purpose.

'If you could just focus a little?'

Julius took a swig of beer and smiled for the first time in days. 'Sorry, it's just part of my DNA to pull on threads and wander down…'

He paused and put his pint down, then laughed out loud.

'Got it! Come on, sup up!'

Sup up be damned. If he knew what the first clue was I wasn't waiting a second longer. I grabbed some chips and pulled him towards the main door. As we got to the exit, he grabbed my hand and pulled me along the pavement, steadying me as I slipped on the snow.

'Can anyone overhear us?'

'No, I've got a little static monitor activated.'

'Of course you have. What about the others in the house?'

I paused. I needed his trust, but I also needed back-up. 'Our location is being monitored and this conversation is being recorded. However, that recording is held by me alone. I choose who to share it with and when.'

'But can they listen in? Right now?'

'No, not unless I open up my comms relay.'

Julius seemed to think about it for a second, and I could see the temptation to share his knowledge was overwhelming him.

'Okay then, this is just between you and me for now?'

I nodded and he continued, an excited smile on his face.

'It was when I said DNA, it all clicked. Plus, of course, we were sitting in The Eagle,' he rushed on. 'When we were in school, Charlie had been playing hockey and had got into a row with the girls' hockey captain because he said that women were vastly inferior to men in every way. Obviously, he was just winding her up but was unlucky enough to be overheard by the deputy head. She was something of a formidable character, to whom no one would even whisper the words *weaker sex*. Anyway, as a punishment she made him write an essay on ten women that had either been plagiarised, overlooked or undervalued. Then he had to read out his essay at assembly to the entire year.'

He paused as we waited for the lights to turn red as we continued towards King's College. 'It became a habit during school after that, to shout that we were doing things in honour of those women.' Julius smiled nostalgically, then said, 'Do you know, I had totally forgotten that. One time he led a rugby charge, shouting "For Eleanor and Aquitaine".'

'So, who is Franklin?'

'Rosalind Franklin. She was instrumental in discovering the double helix in DNA, but it was two male colleagues, Crick and Watson, that got the Nobel Prize.'

'And what does the clue mean? Why is she hungry?'

'It's the chronophage. Its nickname is Rosalind!'

We were now stood by the railings outside King's College, and Julius was pointing across the road to some weird-arsed clock that I had seen a few days ago. On the corner of the street, recessed into the wall and behind a large window, was a huge set of golden dials, over a metre wide, ticking and turning like a bizarre clock face. On the edge of the top dial crawled a giant locust-like insect, crunching its way along the cogs of the wheel. We crossed the road and stood with other sightseers, trying to work out what time the blue glowing lights indicated. It was only correct a couple of times a day, which was, apparently, the point. As a concept, I rather liked it. God knows, I viewed timelines from a slightly different angle to that of my fellow onlookers.

'The insect on top of the clock face is a chronophage, an eater of time.' He looked at me, a huge beam plastered across his face. 'She's hungry.'

'Rosalind?'

'That was our nickname for the chronophage, Rosalind!'

I had to admit this seemed probable. 'So, who's *Lucky*? And how should we look them up?'

'No, I think that's wrong. Charlie either deliberately forgot the comma or just left it off, or I didn't spot it. It's not *Look up Lucky*, it's *Look up, Lucky*, with a comma.'

We both tilted our heads. Above the clock on the second floor was a date carved into the brickwork. 1876.

I was suddenly embraced in a huge hug by Julius, who was grinning like a kid and bouncing up and down.

'Bloody hell! That's it! I think I know what that is as well. At least I think I do. Let's go warm up and I'll tell you what I think it means, and you can plan a break-in.'

Really, he hardly knew me, yet he already knew how to flatter me!

Sitting now, we were grinning at each other like hyenas. His pleasure was infectious, and I was revelling in his enjoyment.

'So, what do you think the numbers mean?'

'I think it's the combination for a safe's lock. There's a safe in the provost's rooms in the Chapter House behind King's College, only no one knows what the combination is. Lost in the mists of time.'

'And no one's ever tried to crack it?'

'No, both the current and previous provosts were two of the world's most unimaginative men and didn't bother to investigate. The first said nothing is truly hidden from God's eye, the second simply installed a lock to his desk drawer, promptly making everyone wonder exactly what it was that he needed to hide.'

'And did you ever find out?'

'Yes, as a prank, Charlie broke into the office and returned with a beer mat.'

'I don't get it.'

'The dean was a rabid teetotaller, but locked in the drawer was a flask of whisky, a glass and a variety of beer mats. The man was a closet drinker.'

'Is it illegal for provosts to drink?'

'Nope.'

'So why do that to yourself?'

'Ah, now who can understand the hypocrisy of the human soul? The thing is, it means that at some point he was in the provost's office and may have cracked the safe's combination, and in fact from the postcard clue I would guess that he did.'

'Wouldn't he have told you?'

'Why? We all love a secret, plus how fabulous to have a private safe.'

'But isn't it in someone else's office?'

'Not perfect, I'll grant you. But I bet it added to the spice. Charlie always says…'

Julius paused, and his face fell as he realised he'd got the tense wrong. In amongst all my concerns, I had to remember I was sitting with someone that had just lost a friend to a violent end.

'So, is the provost's office difficult to break into?'

'I doubt the door is even locked, but we don't want anyone walking in whilst we are trying to open the safe, which is why I hope you have some clever ideas up your sleeve.'

I sat back and sipped my stout. It made sense, and breaking-in sounded almost dull. But quite frankly, at this stage in the mission, I could do with dullness. It was time to plan the next step. My gut feeling was that we were close to finding the egg. It made sense that Charlie had placed it somewhere secure when he went to London, and a smart move to send his friend a clue as to its location. I needed to ready the team. If we did find the egg, then we needed to depart immediately.

Julius had explained his idea, and whilst it meant we had to wait an hour or two, I liked the idea of working under the cover of nightfall. Plus, it meant we could have some food before we left. Some people liked to step through the Q Field on an empty stomach. Personally, I couldn't see the point. Plus, the smells from the kitchen were moreish and I'd already seen sticky toffee pudding on the blackboard. I was having some of that. It was a new one on me, and I had no idea what it was, but it sounded divine.

What I needed right now though, was a back door to leave the pub. If I was Paul, left without any technological ways to track us, I'd go back to basics and establish visuals. I'd been scanning the crowds, but so far I hadn't spotted him. That didn't mean he wasn't there though, following our every step. If I could get away from the tourists and students, then he would lose his cover. Having determined that he wasn't in the actual pub, I left Julius and nipped to the loo.

On my return, I told Julius my plan. 'Right, I've found a way out that leads to an alley. When it's time to go I need you to get us to the provost's study via the least crowded routes.' The chances were that Paul wouldn't make a move until we had the egg in our hands, but I needed Julius to be on high alert. Now that we had solved the clue, he ran the risk of being tortured for his knowledge. I ran through various protocols with him.

'If I shout "down", drop to the ground and find cover. If you see me pull my gun, drop to the ground and find cover. If you hear shots—'

'Drop to the ground and find cover?'

Julius' tone didn't seem to suggest he was taking me seriously.

'While I'm dropping to the ground and finding cover, do you think I can do so, in a constructive, manly fashion?'

'I don't care what fashion you do it in so long as you don't get in my way or end up dead. Both options would be hugely unhelpful. If you do choose to die, could you do it after I have retrieved the egg? A failed recovery and a dead civilian will play hell with my performance metrics.'

'I'll try not to spoil your clean-up rate. That's obviously at the top of my priorities.'

I sighed. This wasn't what I needed. We both needed to be alert, not at odds. I was used to telling people what they needed to do, and then they did it. I didn't mind when Clio or Ramin talked back because I valued their insight and experience. Julius had none of that. Clearly, he had native intelligence, but he had zero experience in self-preservation. Plus, it would have been nice to know that my partner was capable of covering my back.

'Sorry.' Inwardly I could almost see Clio rolling her eyes. 'It's just I need to try to keep you alive. It would be easier for me if you had zero agency, but of course, that's not possible. You're scared and sad and trying to deal with those feelings, whilst also being curious and excited. It's a mess. I appreciate that. Let's go get that egg. Then we'll get you back to safety and take it from there. Yes?'

I escorted him to the loos and then called Ramin.

'Track us closely and get ready to move. We are within two hours of the egg's fracture point. I think I know where it is, so we need to be ready to jump. Tell Clio.'

Every minute past the fracture point we would be messing up the timeline, which was a no-no. The egg didn't exist after 7.45 pm. Every minute that it did ran the risk of temporal problems.

The minute we had the egg in our possession, the normal protocol was to step back with the artefact whilst the rest of the team cleared out the HQ location. With Paul gone rogue, we had a dilemma. It was a judgement call, but last night I had instructed the team to leave booby traps in all the IT equipment we had bought, and to rendezvous at the same location and step together. I had to assume that once we had left with the egg, Paul would then ignore Julius and also step back. Although, how the hell he intended to evade arrest, I had no idea. Maybe he had already stepped back and was laying down a pack of lies against us, then legging it? Maybe he'd decided to retire on Beta and become a master thief? Or a shepherd?

My mind was wandering, and it wasn't helping. Paul's defection made no sense, and it was bugging me. I knew I was missing something, and I was hoping that whatever it was would be revealed to me whilst I was quietly reminiscing by the water's edge with a cocktail in my hand, rather than running for my life thinking, 'Oh, that was it!'

Time to get going; one locked safe, one lost egg, one rogue agent.

What could possibly go wrong?

#37 Julius – Beta Earth

Night had fallen when we left the pub. Julius edged past a load of beer barrels stacked in the alley and turned right. Neith walked beside Julius, constantly checking over her shoulder as they moved briskly past other pedestrians. The alley was dimly lit, only pools of light from various doorways showing the way. Whilst she was glad of the darkness, it also gave Paul more shadows to hide in. Each time they opened onto a busy street, they would pause as Neith scoured the area for Paul or any of the hired thugs she had last seen at the church. Only when she was confident the coast was clear would she allow Julius to lead her to the next alley. Eventually, having passed a pile of bins, Julius banged on a large modern fire door and it swung open into the lane, a large pool of light illuminating the alleyway. A kitchen porter peered out at Julius, then grinned when he saw Neith.

'No pass for your visitor, Professor?'

'Guilty as charged. Let us in and I'll put in a good word for you with Jane.'

Slipping in through the kitchen, the pair dodged around the large pans, readied for the evening meal. Getting into the colleges during term time could be tricky if you didn't have a pass. The porters on the main gates were always alert to the proper security passes. Some porters were more forgiving of a professor signing a visitor into their own college, but King's wasn't Julius' college, and he knew the porter on the main gate was a stickler for rules and regulations. He also didn't think Neith would enjoy standing around like an exposed target whilst the porter tried to deliver a sermon on the importance of his job. He was concerned Neith might take matters into her own hands, and he didn't think Old Barnaby deserved that. This seemed like the quicker option.

Moving from the kitchens through to the dining room, Neith's jaw dropped. The beauty of the room was overwhelming. The long oak tables were fully laid with white linen tablecloths, on top of which sat crystal glasses and china plates. Candles stood flickering on the tables, and the effect was opulent and comforting. The room itself was huge, with a high vaulted ceiling, and decorative mouldings framing large stained glass windows.

'This is a student dining room?'

'High table. King's is known for being a bit OTT. Come on, through here. The provost will be coming down for food in a minute and then the coast will be clear.'

They headed off down oak-lined corridors, passing students beginning to mill around and ready for their supper. Julius decided to loiter down one of the side corridors. The provost's wing was quiet and private, and it would be easy to be spotted.

'Exactly how will I be breaking-in, when you seem to have this covered?'

Julius shrugged. 'You know, when it goes wrong you can jump in and do your thing. We should have the place to ourselves, but you never know.'

Finally, Julius saw the provost emerge along the corridor and hail a few professors as he led the way into dinner.

'Come on.'

Moving at a relaxed pace, Julius headed towards the provost's private study. It was always best to act with confidence, as lurking tended to catch someone's eye. He was relieved to see that Neith had also adopted an air of ownership and was acting as though she had every right to be in here.

As they entered the room, Neith knelt by the skirting board in the corridor before closing the door behind them.

'It'll give us a little heads up if anyone approaches the door.'

Julius winked at her. 'See, that's what I meant by *tricks up your sleeve*. At some point, you and I are going to have a long talk about exactly who you work for.'

Julius moved towards the back of the large mahogany desk and started to lift the edges of the rug.

'Charlie said this safe was set into the floor by the desk. Knowing our luck the desk will be on top of it.' He moved to the other end of the rug and then exhaled in delight. 'No, here it is. Good old Charlie.' Pulling up the wooden trapdoor, he looked down in dismay at the floor safe itself. As expected, there was a locked safe with a set of numbered tumblers by the handle.

'Hell!'

'What's the problem?' Neith had been checking out the room's other doors and windows, ready to make a quick exit. 'Move over, oh…'

Neith's voice trailed off. They had four digits, but this was a six-digit safe. 'Bugger.'

The pair of them looked at each other.

'Any bright ideas?' asked Julius as he tried the four numbers he had and then tried to replicate some of those numbers to fill up the two extra spaces. It was a weak idea, and it wasn't working.

'Look up, Lucky,' said Neith thoughtfully. 'That's the bit of the clue that referred to the safe combination. Maybe the word *Lucky* provides the other two digits? Think Julius, what could *Lucky* mean to Charlie?'

'What about fourteen? It was his favourite number on the rugby pitch. Said it made him lucky. It was a joke because we nearly always lost. But it's a bit obvious.'

'Only to you. Remember, Charlie wrote this message for you and you alone.'

Julius sat back and watched as Neith turned the dials 1, 4.

'No wait,' Julius said, stopping her, 'the clue said, *Look up, Lucky*, so the 1876 first and then fourteen.'

Neith nodded and moved the number on from 4 to 8, and continued with 7,6,1, and finally 4. As the sixth tumbler clicked in, Neith paused and looked at Julius.

'Ready?' she asked, then twisted the handle and pulled up the door.

Sitting in the middle of the safe was a round object wrapped in a tea towel. Leaning forward, Julius carefully placed his hand around the package and lifted it out.

'It's heavy!' Gently, holding the item in one hand, he pulled back the tea towel with the other hand. The pair of them stared in awe at an enamelled egg, featuring St Basil's basilica sitting on a base of pearls and diamonds.

'Wow,' said Neith, 'that has to be one of the most perfect things I have ever retrieved.'

'Still not worth dying for.'

Neith glanced across at Julius. 'No, I'll give you that.' Gathering her wits, Neith was suddenly all action. 'Right, let's get this thing safe.'

From her backpack, she pulled out a container that looked a lot like a child's sturdy lunchbox. Opening it up, she placed the egg alongside a carved red stone; both were lying on a specially moulded base that seemed to cradle the artefacts.

Julius looked at the stone with suspicion. 'Is that an image of Tsarevich Alexei? Have you had the hidden treasure all this time?'

'I'll explain later. Trust me.'

Julius was beginning to feel uneasy. This complete stranger was asking him to trust her, but he realised that he knew absolutely nothing about her. Up until now, he hadn't much cared about the egg. It had been an abstract construct. Something to keep him busy whilst he mourned Charlie. But now, sitting here looking at it, he realised that he cared very much about the egg. He didn't want it to disappear into some private collection. Especially as it was indeed a previously unknown design.

'Neith, I'm not sure about this.'

Ignoring him, Neith clamped the box shut, put it back in her backpack, then cuffed the backpack via a tether to her wrist. Tapping her wrist brace, she spoke into it.

'Team. The parcel is secure. We need to leave now. Ramin, find me somewhere open and dark nearby where we can meet. I don't want any more surprises, and I want us all leaving together.'

She listened to her head-piece then turned to Julius.

'We're leaving now. Can you get me to the back lawn? When I've gone, you'll find a letter from me explaining everything, and there's a finder's fee in your bank account. Come on, let's go. Time's running out.'

Julius wanted to protest. He wanted Charlie back, he wanted to spend more time with Neith. What he said instead was, 'That egg belongs in a museum.'

Neith turned and kissed him, a broad grin on her face. 'I agree, and it will be. The best in the world. Now run!'

Surprised by the kiss, Julius had to race to catch up with her. Looking back, she urged him to keep up.

'Paul may have already left, but once he knows we've gone and the egg has gone, you'll be safe.'

Julius leant on a heavy wooden door. 'Through here, it's quicker,' he said, and suddenly they were outside in the cold, biting air. 'Turn left,' he called to her as she ran ahead.

'It's blocked. Maintenance,'

'Okay, along here and we'll turn left at the chapel.' As she had to backtrack, Julius was briefly leading the way. But then Neith passed him, running along the gravel path as he sprinted to catch up. The pair turned and the path opened into a large grassy quadrant. The lawn was lined by dimly-lit ancient buildings on three sides and a river on the fourth. Two bridges crossed at each corner on the other side of the square.

#38 Neith – Beta Earth

I checked my wrist brace and saw Clio and Ramin were approaching from different corners. Turning to Julius, I realised I was going to miss him.

'It's time for you to go,' I said, frowning. I could hear a motorboat approaching. That was all I needed, witnesses. I could release a wow bang if necessary, but that was a bit ugly, and I tended to prefer a more refined exit. Nice and quiet, no drama. Plus, I would rather spare Julius two mind-altering hits in the same week.

'Seriously, Julius. Go quickly.'

As I stepped forward to give him a hug, a bullet whizzed past my ear and things began to go wrong very fast. It looked like we were gearing up for a dramatic exit after all.

From out of the shadows, I saw Paul running towards me, shouting my name. Ramin was closest to him and was gaining on him. It looked like Ramin must have been tailing Paul as he ran to catch him up, but in the low sodium lighting, I couldn't see properly.

Scanning the quadrant for other threats I saw that the boat had docked. A team of men had spilled out and were running up the bank, all with guns raised. That would explain the bloody bullet. I quickly returned a hail of laser fire to slow some of them down, and tried to work out what the hell was going on. From the far corner near one of the bridges, Clio was running towards the boat team, her own arm outstretched.

As far as I could tell I had two threats, both heading in my direction from opposite corners. I was just about to pull Julius back down the path when I caught the tone of Paul's voice. It was desperate, almost pleading, but not aggressive. I looked to see if the others had registered the unusual tone, whilst I shouted at Julius to get down.

Upon Paul's shout, I watched as Clio changed direction as she began to run towards him. Her long dark frame sprinted across the lawn, and she raised her second arm to steady her shooting arm and fired at Paul. Spinning backwards, he fell into Ramin's arms.

Both Ramin and Paul were on the floor. Ramin was trying to support Paul, and holding him in one arm, he brought up his laser and seemed to be firing in Clio's direction. For a split second, I was paralysed, as my team appeared to be shooting at each other and I didn't know which one to stop.

I aimed my gun at Ramin just as Clio fell forward, shots hitting her in the back from the team that had left the boat. In my ear, I heard Ramin screaming at me to Step. We were two team members down and heavily outgunned. Julius shouted as a bullet tore through the sleeve of his jacket, and left me with no options. Hitting the Step code on my wrist brace, I grabbed Julius and disappeared.

#39 Neith – Alpha Earth

I fell onto the floor of the Step Chamber and vomited copiously. I hadn't done that since I was a rookie, but then I had never carried a human through the Step with me. My ears were ringing, and I felt lightheaded. The security lights were flashing and the sirens blaring. I was still holding Julius' hand and I was relieved to note it was still attached to his whole body, although blood was pouring down his arm. I let go and was even more relieved to find that we hadn't melded into each other. Those essays about the pitfalls of stepping through with other life forms were fun to write up as students, but not so much when you actually did it. At least I would be spared from the "Look at me, kids" lecture circuit.

Some chimeras were operated on, and appendages were removed, mostly tails or ears. When the changes took place at a molecular level, they couldn't be unspliced. Some died instantly as the original body couldn't cope with the trauma, whilst some learnt to live with their new bodies.

I grabbed his wrist again and checked for a pulse before everyone started to run towards us. He was alive but unconscious. Which was more than could be said for Paul. Ramin was sitting beside him, crying. He hadn't thrown up, and I wondered if that was because Paul was already dead when Ramin had stepped through with him? Maybe he'd activated Paul's emergency recall cord before he died? Where was Clio?

Someone shook my shoulder, and I saw Sam trying to speak to me. I couldn't hear him over the noise in my ears and the sirens, but I knew I needed to tell him about Clio.

'Clio fell. Someone shot her. Sam, I couldn't get to her. You need to activate her emergency recall cord.'

He flinched as a medic jabbed something in my arm. The queasiness and ringing began to die down. A team of medics ran in and put Julius on a stretcher, then left quickly. Another team was attending to Ramin and had placed a simple white sheet over Paul's face.

'She fell, trying to save me. Paul was going to kill me.'

'Neith. Don't say anything more. You need to go to the infirmary. You and Ramin can report in due course.'

I tried again. 'Sam. Hit the recall brace. Get Clio back.'

'Neith. We did that the minute you all stepped through. Nothing happened, Neith. Clio's dead.'

I looked at him in horror. 'Sam, she can't be. Try again. She was trying to save me. Try again!'

I couldn't make sense of the situation. My head was pounding, and the room kept tilting. It was impossible that Clio was dead but I knew that the Q Field couldn't handle an inanimate object. If Clio's brace had failed to detect any brain activity, it would simply disengage. I knew the science, but that wasn't helping right now.

Because right now, there was no way that my best friend was dead.

'Sir. Please, Sam, keep trying.'

I could see a commotion amongst the technicians standing around us as someone shouldered their way through.

'What is the meaning of all this shouting? Curator, control yourself. Have you successfully retrieved the egg?'

The egg? I looked up at Chancellor Soliman Alvarez in disbelief. 'Fuck the egg!'

'Sir,' said Sam, stepping between me and the chancellor, 'we have just had a catastrophic incident. This isn't the time or place.'

'I'm in charge of this facility, or have you forgotten?' Alvarez loomed into my view again. 'Have you or have you not got the egg? Have you completely ballsed up your mission?'

Too distressed to argue any more, I tapped the security cuff on my wrist, and technicians stepped forward, tentatively waiting for permission to release it.

'Good,' he boomed, 'at least you haven't screwed up entirely. Give me the release codes and we'll secure it immediately.'

I tried to tell him what they were, but I suddenly had an overwhelming urge to fold my socks. And then I fainted.

When I came around I was lying in the medical bay in the infirmary. There were two armed guards outside my room, and various nurses playing with tubes and wires. A mind mesh was attached to my skull and various drips were plugged into my arms. As I looked across the bed, Sam was sitting beside me. As was the chancellor.

'Report, Curator!' he barked. 'What are your release codes?'

The second pair of guards standing behind him tightened their lips. We knew each other, we all did, and I would have been equally revolted to see an injured curator being treated like this. It was a biometric lock plus code. I released it and asked Sam to open the case so that I could see it was undamaged. We all looked at it in awe. It was a thing of beauty. As I leant forward to touch it, Alvarez snapped the box shut and took possession of it.

'Sir, two Alphas died for that. I want their names to be recorded alongside its display card in the museum.'

'Quantum Curator Salah, you are the disgraced leader in a botched mission. You are in no position to tell me to do anything.' With that, he left the room with the case and the two guards. A further two remained at my door.

'Are those two guards there for my protection or detention?'

'Protection. But if you can bear the ignominy, I'm telling everyone they are for your detention. Something went badly wrong on this mission, and I need to find out what. You and Ramin are my only witnesses.'

'What about Julius and the angel?'

'The angel disappeared. They were kidnapped on arrival. Their kidnapper was killed, and we have no trace of them.'

'Fuck. But that means Paul had back-up. He hadn't gone rogue.'

'I need to know more. I've debriefed Ramin, and your Beta is in a medically induced coma until the medics are happy with his vitals. I need your version of the events.'

And so I told him the whole sorry mess as I saw it. As I finished Dr Giovanetti, the infirmary director, entered the room.

'Okay, Sam, I need her now.'

'How bad is it?' asked Sam.

'Not bad at all actually, but how about I tell her first? Hmm?' he muttered, smiling.

Well, that didn't sound good. Especially as I felt fine. Well, groggy, and I kept wanting to fold socks, but other than that, fine. I was trying to block all thoughts of Clio out of my mind. I would deal with my grief in private. Not here, with armed guards watching me and nurses coming to and fro, checking on my vitals.

As he got up to leave, Sam totally alarmed me by leaning over and giving me a huge hug. Then he left the room without saying a word. I watched him go then turned back to the head of the infirmary. That in itself wasn't a good sign.

'Am I dying?'

Dr Giovanetti laughed. 'No, you're fine. I just think you put Sam through the wringer. He cares about all of you, and losing two has been hellish for him. You had a very narrow escape.'

'Is this about Stepping with Julius?'

'Yes, you've had a few splicing issues.'

Oh crap. I looked at him in alarm and tried to assess my body. It all looked and felt normal.

'What "issues"?'

He handed me a mirror, and as I looked into it a quizzical eyebrow and a blue iris peered back at me. They looked as surprised as I felt. My right eyebrow and iris were the same as normal. My left side were Julius'. I gently touched the new eyebrow, which felt thicker and bushier than my own smooth brows.

'Man, my tweezers are going to be busy!'

'That's the spirit.' He smiled at me kindly. 'Now, we can do a graft and fix your eyebrow, but the iris is staying blue. We can sort out some contacts for you. You may also be experiencing some neural splicing?'

'Is that the socks thing?'

He asked me to explain, and I told him that I kept feeling an urge to fold socks. I don't even own any.

'Okay. Let's keep an eye on that. Any other odd thoughts or memories, jot them down. Hopefully, they will begin to fade. But it's good to record and monitor these things so that we can learn from them.'

Which reminded me. 'Am I now going to have to attend the college "Show and Tell" circuit?' I groaned when he grinned at me.

I couldn't wait to tell Clio. Oh boy, she was going to rip the piss out of me…

And then the reality of the past few hours hit me like a plank in the face. I suddenly doubled up in the pain of my grief, and, as I cried, I remembered outrunning crocodiles with her, dancing at the local bar and cheering together at the end of rugby matches. Rugby matches weren't my memory, however, and I realised I was also experiencing Julius' grief for Charlie. Waving the doctor away, I turned my face to the wall and tried to go to sleep.

#40 Neith – Alpha Earth

The following day I awoke with all sense of Step nausea gone. There was nothing to be done about my eye for now, and odd sock-related incidents were being monitored. I wanted to see Julius, not just to ask him about his socks thing, but because I wanted to be there when he woke up. He had a lot to take on board and I wanted to help him with it. After all, it was my fault he was here.

When I asked if I could see him, I was told he had been moved to another department and was still in a coma. I was still arguing with them when Sam arrived in full formal dress and told me that I was being invited to attend a review panel. I think the word *invited* was just a pleasantry. I was escorted there by the two guards, who Sam had assured me were there to protect me. But neither would make eye contact with me, and I felt distinctly unprotected. Outside the hearing chamber, I saw Ramin waiting, similarly flanked by two guards, and I rushed over to hug him. For a few minutes, all we could do was hug each other. Then he stepped back and touched my eyebrow.

'My, you have let yourself go! Very Beta chic!'

Crap joke, but it made me laugh. We held hands while we sat down. An official told us we weren't to talk to each other, so we just squeezed each other's hand instead and wondered what lay in store for us.

As we were called into the hearing, we faced a panel of seven individuals all seated behind a long table on a raised dais. Cameras were set up in the corners to record the interview, but no people were seated in the audience chambers. I also noticed there were no chairs for us. I raised my eyebrow at Ramin, who just giggled. I decided to take the skin graft. If my sardonic twitch of the eyebrow was going to simply make people laugh, I would have to fix that. However, Ramin laughing was just the stiffener I needed as we stood and faced the panel.

Director Ranai al-Cavifi sat in the middle of seven officials. The director was head of the civil agency and was in overall charge of the township of Greater Alexandria. She was responsible for the daily welfare of ten million citizens and was a very popular leader. This was her third term in office. Mostly I respected the woman, but this was the first time I had ever met her. Sitting on either side of her I recognised Chancellor Asha Giovanetti, head of security and Chancellor Soliman Alvarez, head of the Q Facility. The other faces were unfamiliar, and not introduced.

The director stood up and cleared her voice to open the hearing. Halfway through her opening address, I cut her off.

'Is your seat comfortable?'

'I beg your pardon?'

'I asked if your seat was comfortable, Director. Only *ours* aren't. Yesterday we came through a Q Field at high speed. I sustained splice injuries in the line of service, and Ramin here held his friend as he died. I witnessed my best friend die in front of me and was forced to leave her body behind. Despite all this, we retrieved the artefact in one piece and without any damage whatsoever to the inanimate object. So, I ask again. Is your chair comfortable, and does your water taste nice?'

The proceedings were delayed for a few moments as two chairs and a pitcher of water were brought in.

Director al-Cavifi looked at me coldly and asked if I was happy for her to proceed. I nodded.

The questioning went back and forth as we were cross-examined. The panel appeared unhappy with every step of our retrieval. It was hard not to take this personally.

'Explain how QC Flint died.'

'I don't understand myself. Clio—'

'This is a formal investigation, so please refer to their titles. QC will suffice instead of quantum curator.'

I bit my lip. Everything about this was being engineered to make us feel uncomfortable. Someone was clearly being lined up for the chop, and I had a feeling that someone was me.

'Apologies. QC Clio Masoud aimed her gun at QC Paul Flint as he charged towards me. But laser fire should have only stunned him. Not killed him.'

'Are you sure of that?'

'Completely.'

'Only, we did an autopsy on QC Flint, and he was shot with a bullet, not a laser.'

I paused and thought it through.

'I saw Ramin, sorry, QC Gamal, running towards QC Flint, his laser drawn, but by his side. I then saw QC Masoud raise her weapon and point it at QC Flint, who then fell to the ground. There were men running up from the riverbank. I could hear shots. It is my analysis that Clio shot Paul, thereby saving my life.'

'Please, QC Salah—Neith—I understand this is difficult for you, and we are sympathetic to your situation, but we need you to remain formal.'

She smiled at me, and for the first time, I sensed a bit of human warmth coming from her. Maybe I had misread the situation? Maybe I wasn't for the chop? Gratefully, I nodded my head in acknowledgement, and she proceeded.

'Was it possible that QC Flint was shot by the men on the riverbank? The night was dark, the situation was heightened. It would have been easy to confuse the trajectory of two similar shots.'

Relived, I felt some tension leave my shoulders. I had been worrying about that point. I could understand Clio halting Paul, but not killing him.

'Yes, Director al-Cavifi. That could be an acceptable interpretation.'

The questioning continued.

'When you were in Charles Bradshaw's house you said you heard the two Betas refer to a "scary woman" who seemed to be running the show?'

'Yes.'

'And, do you have any idea who this may have been?'

'No.'

'Did you get the impression that this female was Alpha or Beta?'

'Alpha.'

'Because?'

'Because whoever was running the show was constantly one step ahead of us. I didn't think a Beta team would have been capable of outfoxing us. Unless Beta Earth knows about Alpha's existence? I was under the impression that they don't?' I watched as the panel smiled dismissively and continued. 'I now know the other team were ahead of us because QC Flint was feeding them information. QC Flint has never visited that timeline, so he wouldn't have been able to have established Beta connections. Therefore, this female was Alpha.'

'Well, you see our problem with that then?'

'No.' Well I did, but I was going to make them spell it out because frankly, I didn't like where they were going with it and I wanted to challenge them about it directly.

'There were only two Alpha females on Beta Earth at that timeframe.'

I paused. I was damned if I did and damned if I didn't, but if I didn't speak now, there would always be whispers about me behind my back.

'The only reference to a female operative was heard by me and Julius. Why would I needlessly volunteer this information to you, knowing it would incriminate me?'

'Well then, that leaves us with QC Masoud as the unknown operative.'

I flushed. I knew they were going to try to pin it on her, but it still hurt to hear it. Especially as she was no longer able to defend herself.

'I resent that implication and want it struck from the record. It was enough that she died in the line of duty. She died saving us. She died, and we left her body behind, but for you to cast a slur on her name is the final insult. If those allegations are not withdrawn, I shall refuse to continue with this inquisition.'

'This is hardly an inquisition. We simply need to get to the facts. In light of what we have just discussed, is it possible that the woman those men referred to could have been a Beta? Maybe one that had been hired by QC Flint to act as his intermediary?'

I conceded that it was a possibility. In fact, the more I thought about it the more I liked it.

After thanking me for my report, the team now moved on to Ramin.

'Quantum Curator Gamal, when QC Salah and Julius Strathclyde went in pursuit of the clue, QC Salah gave you a command. What was that?'

'To inform QC Masoud that we had switched on Julius' tracker and that they were off to search for the clue.'

'And what did you do?'

'I told her that they were going to visit Julius' work colleagues.'

'And did you tell her that Julius had a tracker on?'

'No.'

I looked at Ramin in surprise as he stared straight ahead, giving his report unblinking. I knew he'd been having concerns about the team, but I hadn't realised he had been actively trying to keep Clio out of the loop. The panel looked as surprised as I felt, and continued their questioning.

'No? Can I ask why you ignored a direct instruction from your team leader?'

'Because I no longer trusted QC Masoud and I didn't want her to know that Julius was protected. I also wanted to see if she would try to go after him again.'

'Again?'

'Yes, I believe she had tried to have him snatched at the church service.'

'Ramin! That's not possible—'

'QC Salah, please don't interrupt. QC Gamal, would you proceed to explain your concerns.'

I sat and listened in horror as Ramin tried to destroy Clio's reputation. Each time I thought I could see a way to argue her corner, Ramin heaped on another piece of damning evidence.

'Is it possible that in your failure to realise that your teammate was a traitor, you are looking to lay the blame on someone else? Namely, a team member that gave her life in the line of her duty to save her unit.'

This was all wrong. Why were they attacking Ramin? Why was he attacking Clio? Why couldn't he simply accept that Paul had betrayed all of us?

'Ramin. Let it go. Paul let us all down. We don't know why, but—'

'I do.'

'Stop,' said the director. 'You've already reported on this in an earlier deposition. The matter is in hand.'

I looked from the panel and back to Ramin. 'What are you talking about?'

'Gamal, may I remind you that that is classified information.'

'Neith deserves to know Paul's dying words.'

'I'm warning you.'

Ramin turned in his chair and held my hand. 'Neith, Paul's dying words were "Save my sister".'

The director stood up. 'QC Ramin Gamal, for breaching classified information and for trying to besmirch the reputation of a fallen colleague, we are placing you on six months sand leave.'

I gasped. Sand leave was basically one step away from being fired for gross negligence. Reduced pay, reduced privileges, reduced workload. Sand leave was nearly always followed by a quiet dismissal. It was a terrible punishment and not one that Ramin deserved.

'Director! That's unfair.' I protested to al-Cavifi but made eye contact with everyone seated on the panel. Hopefully, I could convince some of them to intercede. 'Ramin was simply reporting the facts as he saw them.' I didn't understand why he was trying to blame Clio and protect Paul, but sand leave? No way.

'QC Salah, that's enough. Captain Nymens, please escort QC Gamal to his desk.'

I pushed my chair back. This was ridiculous. If anyone was responsible for the team's failings, it was me. I couldn't bear to hear him denigrate Clio, but this wasn't right either. And what was going on with Paul's sister? I hadn't even realised that Sam was in the room, and wondered when he had entered. Now he stepped forward and lightly placed his hand on Ramin's elbow. Both men ignored me as they left the room. Things seemed to have suddenly spiralled out of control.

'QC Salah. This committee finds you innocent of any mismanagement of the retrieval of Case Number FE 988776. We consider, in light of the extreme interference that you experienced, that a successful retrieval went above and beyond our expectations of you. You have our highest recommendations and you will be awarded the Merit of Alexander.'

With that, the seven rose and began to head out of a side door. I couldn't stand it. This was all wrong, and I moved to intercept the director. Chancellor Soliman tried to brush me away, but al-Cavifi turned and dismissed the others until we were alone in the room.

'I don't want the Merit. I want answers.'

Al-Cavifi looked at me sadly. 'Regretfully, I can't give you many. Much of what has happened has been above your clearance level. Suffice it to say, we found Paul's sister, and she was alive and well. We have not found your angel, sadly. We have no evidence that Ramin was working with Paul, but we're keeping an eye on him to see if we can flush out his contacts on this side of the Q Field.'

'But none of this makes any sense. Ramin isn't a traitor!'

'Was Clio?'

'No, of course not.'

'And yet Ramin tried to pin the blame on her. I find that very telling, don't you?'

I had no words.

'I have spoken to Captain Nymens and you are to be given a month's paid leave. You need it, but more importantly, you deserve it. As soon as the egg has been unveiled, I don't expect to see you again until you are fully recovered. I don't need to tell you how incredibly proud we all are of you right now.'

With that final accolade, she left the room. I stood alone. Had any victory ever felt more hollow?

#41 Sam & Ramin

'With me, QC Gamal. I'll drive you home.'

'Sam, this is ridiculous. Why am I being put on sand leave?'

Sam said nothing and continued to escort Ramin to his locker. In silence, he watched Ramin grab a few bits and pieces, placing them in his backpack. As he went to pick up a book, Sam stopped him.

'Sorry. No printed material leaves the building.'

'Great Ra, Sam, it's a novel!'

'Don't make this harder than it is. You haven't been fired, which I think you should have been, but the least you can do is do as requested. No written materials to leave the Q Zone.'

Ramin narrowed his eyes. If Sam was going to play the party lapdog, then so be it.

'Right. That's me done then,' he snapped. 'I don't need a lift. Send Neith my love, if it won't kill her!'

'You will have a lift. I was told to see you safely home.'

Ramin stared at Sam in silence. The last forty-eight hours had taken on a nightmarish quality. His friend had died in his arms, and he had uncovered something that seemed to hint at a darker conspiracy. Neith had turned her back on him, and Sam, Sam who always put his curators first, was throwing him out of the building like he was a piece of rubbish.

By now they had reached the opening concourse of the Alexandrian complex then Sam seemed to pat his pockets in a gesture of obvious annoyance.

'Damn. I've left my keys in the office. Taxi!'

A tuk-tuk pulled up. Telling Ramin to get in, he gave the driver Ramin's address and then leant back, closing his eyes and ignoring Ramin. After five minutes, he opened them and shouted to the driver that they would get out here. He said that his friend was going to be sick and that they'd walk the rest of the way.

Ramin watched as the driver re-joined the ranks of rickshaws and tuk-tuks. The longer distance hover-cars flew overhead, and an afternoon breeze blew in off the Mareotis lagoon. They were still a good mile from his house, but at the moment he felt like a walk was a good idea. He would have preferred to be alone, though.

'Right. Sorry about that.' Sam took a deep breath. 'Ramin, I believe you.'

Ramin looked out over the water and was startled by the sudden tears in his eyes. He brushed them away. If he was going to cry it would be for Paul, not himself.

'What's with all the cloak and dagger stuff, pretending not to have your car keys? You always keep your keys in the car's sun visor.'

'Walls have ears and cars might as well. I don't know who might be listening.' He went on to explain what he and Asha had discovered when she had run through the security cameras. 'Someone is watching things. And I think it's the same people that were behind Clio and Paul.'

'People?'

'Yes. Whatever this is, and I have no idea what's going on or why, more than one person is involved, and they are at a higher level than me.'

'So, you believe me that Clio was dirty?'

'Yes. It's the only explanation that fits the evidence.'

'So why was Paul involved? What happened with his sister?'

'The director was right. When you first mentioned her in your initial debrief, we went to check and she was absolutely fine. She had no idea what we were talking about.'

'But they were his dying words, Sam. He wouldn't have wasted his breath on a lie. She was the most important thing in the world to him.'

'Exactly. I believe that Paul must've been shown a faked video of his sister being kidnapped or tortured.'

'But why didn't he investigate?'

'Because I think he was already on Beta Earth at that stage and there was no way for him to verify it. Only three people on Beta would've been able to show him that video. You pretty much ruled yourself out by telling everyone his last words. I had a hard time imagining Neith doing it, and given everything else you said about Clio in the tribunal…' Sam threw a stone into the water, disturbing the birds. 'Well, that worked for me.'

Ramin watched as the birds flew up into a nearby tree.

'And now she's dead.'

'Yes. But whoever she was working for isn't.'

'I think she was about to shoot you when she got shot in the crossfire.'

'Why not shoot Neith? She had the egg, after all. She could have stepped away at any moment.'

'Neith was protecting Julius. I don't think it occurred to Clio that Neith would do something as dangerous as Step whilst holding another person. The minute she'd released Julius, I suspect Clio would've shot her.'

'Instead, she was shot in the back by her own hired thugs.'

'Seems a fitting way to go.'

'But everyone thinks she's a hero!'

'Good. Until we can reveal the truth, then that's how it stays. But for now, you are in danger. You need to keep your head down and don't rock the boat. Whoever is operating on this side had no problem with killing an orderly that worked for them and who knows what's happened to that frail, defenceless angel. Whoever these people are, they are ruthless.'

'Is Neith safe?'

'So long as she keeps banging on about how brave and wonderful Clio was, then yes.'

Ramin paused, trying to take it all in. The men sat silently whilst an old croc pulled itself out of the water to warm up in the overhead sun. Little birds flew down and landed on its back, pecking away at the bits of mud and weed.

'Why didn't she believe me?'

Sam paused. He knew Ramin wasn't asking about Director al-Cavifi.

'Lots of reasons. Clio was her best friend. She's grieving, and you're asking her to accept that Clio is not only dead but a cold-hearted, manipulative killer. And if she can accept that, then she also has to come to terms with the fact that she was totally fooled, and her mission failed because she trusted an enemy.'

#42 Neith – Alpha Earth

The sun was beginning to set over the sea as the visiting dignitaries stood on the marble plaza sipping champagne whilst waiting for the grand ceremony.

'Did you know this tastes just the same as the stuff at home?'

I grinned. Every day with Julius was a constant litany of what was the same and what was different. It had only been a week, but he was adapting pretty well. It had helped when we had shown him the library. Earlier in the day, Paul had been buried whilst Clio received a full ceremonial dispatch with honours. There was obviously nothing to bury, but her name was engraved on the wall for fallen heroes. I'd have rather had her here by my side, but at least I could stand proud knowing that I had been her partner.

This evening's event was to launch the new acquisition: an undiscovered Fabergé egg. I had promised Julius that it would be going to the world's greatest museum, and here it was in the Mouseion of Alexandria. Julius and I were given pride of place as the egg was revealed. Of course, the actual egg was stored in a hermetic vault, but in front of us was a perfect 3D printed replica.

'So, someone sitting in New York can dial this up and hold a copy for themselves?'

'Yes,' I said, and smiled. It seemed funny explaining something that a seven-year-old knew inside out.

'And they wouldn't be able to tell the difference? Everything moves and feels the same?'

'Identical. Except for the fact it dissolves into its nano parts after a couple of hours. That, and the "Nano" stamped across its side.'

'What if I wanted to study it for longer?'

'Then just order a hologram. Use the printer if you need to hold it.'

'And anyone can do that, no restrictions, no limits, no requisition chits?'

I knew that Julius was soon going to be living in the holo labs. 'Pay attention, it's almost ready.'

'It's a shame Ramin can't be here.'

I glared at Julius. Nothing was going to spoil today. This ceremony, the earlier memorial, everything was to honour Clio.

'That wouldn't be appropriate.'

As the lights went down, a spotlight focussed on the white-gloved hands of a curator as she removed the egg from its box to a gasp from the audience and a huge burst of applause. As she twisted off the first egg top, those lucky enough to be standing nearby saw the beautiful portraits of a Tsar and Tsarina gazing lovingly at each other. Those further back looked up at the holo projections, while those at home or in cafés and bars were watching on live feeds. This was a huge event and was breaking all records for audience figures.

And why wouldn't it? The tale of its retrieval was the stuff of a Beta drama. Violence, betrayal, greed, gunfights, and that was just the Romanovs. Add in Fabergé and the curators, and it was a perfect storm. Of course, the full story had been gently doctored. No point in alarming the general public.

As the curator continued to reveal each smaller egg, the world watched in wonder, until the final ruby intaglio was revealed, and the audience once again burst into applause.

As the fireworks died down, Director al-Cavifi stepped forward and addressed the audience.

'As you know, we always attach full details to every artefact about the retrieval team involved in this. However, this time we have a couple of extra names to add.'

I squeezed Julius' hand. Sam had asked me about this idea when it had first been suggested. I'd agreed wholeheartedly but hadn't said anything in case it didn't happen.

'We always honour the Beta creators whose works we save and treasure, but today we're also going to honour two Betas who helped secure this lost Fabergé masterpiece. Charles Bradshaw and Julius Strathclyde. I think we can say beyond a shadow of a doubt that here is a Julius we can all celebrate.'

Cheers and laughter floated out over the warm evening air. The director stepped forward again, raising her glass. 'Ladies and gentlemen. To the Mouseion of

Alexandria, to the illustrious men and women of the Q Field, and finally, to Julius Strathclyde and team leader, Neith Salah.'

'To Julius and Neith.'

The toast was taken up and rang out over the towers and parks.

Neith and Julius just looked at each other and shrugged, two perfectly mismatched eyes grinning back at each other.

Interlude 5

The following text conversation was retrieved doing a sweep of the ghost files of the Q Zone security system. It has been added to the evidence report for Case No: 234530/H. As yet neither correspondent has been identified.

- My companions are not happy with your failure.

- We retrieved the egg!

- Fool. Do you think there is any way that we can counterfeit it now? With all your ridiculous mismanagement of the incident, we have been forced to let it go.

- I still insist I handled the situation as well as possible.

- Rubbish. Captain Nymens now suspects you and we can hardly move against him without tipping our hand. If you do anything to make him suspect you further rest assured that you will be on your own.

#The End

The woman wiped the mud off her knees and tried to wipe clean her palms on the thighs of her trouser. She sighed deeply and swore. Now she was going to have to hunker down and wait until someone came to get her. She heard sirens getting closer; their lights flashing in the dark skies. That was her cue to leave, and she walked over to the bridge and waited with the crowd that was beginning to gather. All around her people speculated excitedly. Had she seen anything? Was that gunfire? Had she heard anything?

Stupid bloody shit flies. Time to go and find some French Fancies whilst she waited to be evacuated.

Read On...

Book Two

The Quantum Curators and the Enemy Within

Order now

Want to read more?

If you can't wait, the first few pages are at the end of this book.

Acknowledgements

It's easy to think of an author writing in some splendid isolation. Scribbling away in a fabulous den or some book-lined study. Usually though, they are clearing a space at the kitchen table, shouting at the children or grabbing five minutes at the end of work. Alternatively, they are jotting down great ideas whilst they're out shopping, then getting home and wondering what that unintelligible scrawl was supposed to signify.

Or at least that's me. So, I am hugely grateful to two of my friends, Anna and Alexandra, and to Steve, my husband. I want to thank them for their reading of each draft and their encouragement at every step of the way. I am also grateful that any eye-rolling over my constant pleas for reassurance, was done behind my back.

A special thanks also goes to Alexandra who came away with me for a small writing break, where she helped me shape the series.

You are going to love what comes next…

Hello and thank you

Getting to know my readers is really rewarding, I get to know more about you and enjoy your feedback; it only seems fair that you get something in return, so if you sign up for my newsletter you will get various free downloads, depending on what I am currently working on, plus advance notice of new releases. I don't send out many newsletters, and I will never share your details. If this sounds good, visit the following:

https://www.thequantumcurators.com

I'm also on all the regular social media platforms so look me up.

@thequantumcurators

Did you enjoy this book?

You can make a big difference.

Reviews are powerful and can help me build my audience. Independent authors have a much closer relationship with their readers, and we survive and thrive with your help.

If you've enjoyed this book, then please let others know or leave a review online.

Thank you for helping!

Now, Read on…

The Quantum Curators and the Enemy Within

Chapter One

My name is Julius Strathclyde and I might be dead. This is my story.

I waded through the freezing water. People surged past me crying, others grabbed my arm demanding to know if the way ahead was blocked. Their voices bounced weirdly off the rising water levels and flock-lined corridors. An old lady in a beautiful chiffon gown held a small lapdog aloft, a fur stole wrapped around the top of them in some futile attempt to stay warm. I removed my dinner jacket and draped it over her shoulders, tucking the stole underneath. The dog snapped at me, but she scolded it and pleaded with me to help. We began to make our way to the outer deck when I remembered my mission. She held on to me, begging me not to abandon her. Ignoring her cries, I turned and fought against the tide of other first-class passengers, struggling through the water. A man pushed past, ushering his wife and children along. Without my jacket, he had mistaken me for staff. Or maybe he had spotted my shoes earlier in the salon. I had tried to explain I needed Oxfords, not brogues, but the guys back at base hadn't believed that such a minor issue would be important. But maybe they had a point, given that I was up to my waist in Arctic water.

I struggled past the crowd until their voices fell away and continued marking the cabin door numbers. Twelve, thirteen, fourteen, the floor shuddered and I felt the boat tilt further. I could hear distant screams and shouts, somewhere a violin was playing, but here in this corridor, all was quiet. Just strange mechanical groans echoing along the structure, the water muffling everything else. My shoes slipped on the carpet and I had to grab onto the balustrade, my arm plunged into the water, and I could see goosefleshed skin through my sopping sleeve. As I got to Cabin 15, I tried the door, but ridiculously it was locked. Who, whilst fleeing for their life on a sinking ship, locks the door? I went to pull out my lock picks and realised with horror that they were nice and safe in my jacket pocket, which was now on its way to the lifeboats.

Feeling a little foolish, I saw I would have to open the door with brute force. Running at it wouldn't work as the water was now waist level. I tried the door handle again, just in case. Definitely locked. The lights on the wall sconces flickered. Trying to do this in the dark would be a pain until I remembered my wrist brace and flicked on the torch. When the lights went out, I would be ready. I looked up and down the corridor, which was now empty of people but full of rising water. Strange items floated on the surface, a hairbrush, a child's doll.

At the end stood a solid metal fire extinguisher. Only to be used in case of an emergency. Well, I think this counted.

I hitched it off the wall and returned to the door of Cabin 15, which contained the jewel-encrusted Rubáiyát of Omar Khayyám. The sole reason for my presence.

Heaving the extinguisher out of the water, I smashed it into the upper half of the door. In a rush, the door gave way. I fell into the room as the water from the corridor surged past me, levelling up in the room beyond. My ribs smashed onto a table and I ended up in a heap on the other side of the room, along with the other furniture that had all been swept forward in the wave of water. By the time I got to my feet, the water had equalised and was now up to my chest. I cursed myself; I hadn't anticipated that the door would have kept out so much of the water. My entire body was beginning to shake with the cold, but I had to get to the book. There was a distant metallic groan as the ship twisted further. The floor was now almost at a thirty-degree angle and the water was pouring in through the door. I hopped and swam to the far wall, wrenching the painting away from the wall safe. With shaking fingers I removed my wrist brace and, activating its magnet, placed it against the wall of the safe and turned the dials. The brace confirmed each click. Opening the door, water poured in and hundreds of dollar bills floated out. Grabbing a velvet bag, I shoved it in my trouser pocket and sagged with relief. I could finally get out of here.

'Thief!' I heard the voice as a heavy body slammed me towards the wall, my chest and shoulder hitting the metal door of the safe and forcing the air out of my lungs. I tried to duck but the person behind me had their hand in my hair and their other hand bunched around the neck of my shirt.

'I wondered what you were doing heading away from the lifeboats, and I was right. You're nothing but a dirty little thief.'

Releasing my collar, he grabbed the book from my pocket but of course, this was a mistake. Unpinned and recovering a few seconds of breathing space, I fell in a dead weight. As I did so, I kicked out my back leg and twisted against his leg. The two of us fell into the water. He hadn't been expecting that and it gave me a couple of vital seconds to turn and face him.

It was the man from the corridor that had barged past me earlier. Doubtless, he had got his family on the lifeboats and then returned for his treasures. I couldn't imagine greater stupidity, although as I looked over his shoulder I saw my wrist brace stuck beside the safe and realised my stupidity outstripped his. I was an idiot. How could I get past him, get the brace, and get out of here? I thought I'd try the truth.

'Sir! Listen to me. I'm trying to save it, not steal it.'

He lunged towards me with a roar. So much for trying to reason with him. He was much larger than me but whilst he moved and fought like a street fighter his dinner jacket suggested that it had been a few years since his ill-gotten gains had elevated him from the alleyways to the opera houses. Scratch a gentleman and you'll often find dirt and corruption under your fingernails.

I ducked under his fist and stepped to one side. Fighting in deep water was hampering both of us but his height was lending him a small advantage. I smashed a punch on his nose but wasn't quick enough to avoid a ringing clout to the ear. I slipped under the surface and was wrenched up again as he grabbed my hair. I tried to pull free but as I did the ground under my feet shuddered. He released his grip as the ship tipped and we were both suddenly swimming, the lights flickered once and then went out. I heard him shout out in alarm.

'Where's the door? I'll let you keep the book if you get me out of here.'

I stayed silent, trying to conserve my energy. He was already lost; I didn't want to join him.

The water level was rising quickly, and I was blind, no longer able to tell whether it was a floor, ceiling or wall above my head. I needed to find the safe and get my wrist brace. Swimming forward, I decided that feeling the surface in front of me I might be able to orientate myself. The ship was now no longer filling with water but sinking to the bottom of the ocean. Time was running out. My head hit the top; the room was now almost full of water. I felt above me, and my hands touched an ornate picture frame. This was the one opposite the safe, I was sure of it. The water now rose around my face and I could feel the onset of panic. I was freezing cold and blind and knew that my life was being counted down in seconds. Taking a deep breath, I duck dived and tried to swim down towards the safe and my wrist brace. My throat was becoming painful and my eyes were bulging. I thought my lungs would explode and I drew in a deep breath of water.

Read On...

Made in the USA
Las Vegas, NV
13 September 2022

55209169R10177